First Impressions

A Musical Comedy

Adapted by
Abe Burrows

I0600513

From
Helen Jerome's dramatization of
Jane Austen's Novel,
Pride and Prejudice

Music and Lyrics by
Robert Goldman, Glenn Paxton, and
George Weiss

A SAMUEL FRENCH ACTING EDITION

SAMUEL
FRENCH
FOUNDED 1830
New York Hollywood London Toronto
SAMUELFRENCH.COM

ISBN   978-0-573-66252-2   Printed   in   U.S.A.   #8039

"FIRST IMPRESSIONS"

Adapted by
ABE BURROWS

From

Helen Jerome's dramatization
of
Jane Austen's novel, "Pride and Prejudice"

Music & Lyrics by
ROBERT GOLDMAN—GLENN PAXTON—GEORGE WEISS

CAST OF CHARACTERS
(In Order of Appearance)

MR. BENNET	*Laurie Main*
MARY BENNET	*Lois Bewley*
MRS. BENNET	*Hermione Gingold*
LYDIA BENNET	*Lynn Ross*
KITTY BENNET	*Lauri Peters*
JANE BENNET	*Phyllis Newman*
MAID	*Beverly Jane Welch*
ELIZABETH BENNET	*Polly Bergen*
LADY LUCAS	*Sibyl Bowman*
CHARLOTTE LUCAS	*Ellen Hanley*
CAROLINE BINGLEY	*Marti Stevens*
CHARLES BINGLEY	*Donald Madden*
FITZWILLIAM DARCY	*Farley Granger*
COACHMEN	*Garrett Lewis and John Starkweather*
CAPTAIN WICKHAM	*James Mitchell*
LIEUTENANT DENNY	*Bill Carter*
LIEUTENANT ROCKINGHAM	*Stuart Hodes*
SIR WILLIAM LUCAS	*Richard Bengal*
BUTLER	*Norman Fredericks*
MR. STUBBS	*Casper Roos*
WILLIAMS	*Jay Stern*
COLLINS	*Christopher Hewett*
BUTLER AT ROSINGS	*John Starkweather*
LADY CATHERINE DE BOURGH	*Mary Finney*
LADY ANNE	*Martha Mathes*

MUSICAL NUMBERS

ACT I

1. Five Daughters.
2. I'm Me.
3. Have You Heard the News?
4. A Perfect Evening.
5. As Long as There's a Mother.
6. Jane.
7. Love Will Find Out the Way.
8. A Gentleman.
9. No.
10. I Feel Sorry for the Girl.
11. I Suddenly Find it Agreeable.
12. This Really Isn't Me.
13. Wasn't It a Lovely Wedding.

ACT II

14. Wedding Talk.
15. A House in Town.
16. The Heart Has Won the Game.
17. Let's Fetch the Carriage.

CAST BY SCENES
ACT ONE
SCENE 1

Longbourn
MRS. BENNET
MARY BENNET
ELIZABETH BENNET
JANE
LYDIA
KITTY
Musical Numbers: "Five Daughters"—"I'm Me"

SCENE 2

Longbourn Exterior
MRS. BENNET
MR. BENNET
LADY LUCAS
2 COACHMEN
    STARKWEATHER
    LEWIS
Musical Number: "News"

SCENE 3

Assembly Ball
LADY LUCAS
CHARLOTTE
ELIZABETH
LYDIA
WICKHAM
JANE
DARCY
MISS BINGLEY
MRS. BENNET
SIR WILLIAM
BINGLEY
BUTLER (Fredericks)
MR. STUBBS (Roos)
Musical Numbers: "Perfect Evening"—"Mazurka"

SCENE 4

Longbourn Exterior
MRS. BENNET
MR. BENNET
KITTY

5

JANE
LYDIA
ELIZABETH
Musical Number: "Mother"

SCENE 5

Netherfield
BINGLEY
DARCY
MISS BINGLEY
WILLIAMS (Stern)
ELIZABETH
Musical Numbers: "Jane"—"Love Will Find Way"

SCENE 6

Longbourn Exterior
LYDIA
KITTY
MRS. BENNET
MR. BENNET
JANE
MARY
ELIZABETH
COLLINS
Musical Number: "Five Daughters Reprise"

SCENE 7

Netherfield Garden Party
MRS. BENNET
COLLINS
MISS BINGLEY
DARCY
BINGLEY
JANE
WICKHAM
LADY LUCAS
ELIZABETH
LYDIA
Musical Number: "Sorry for the Girl"

SCENE 8

Garden Party Exterior
COLLINS
DARCY
ELIZABETH
JANE
BINGLEY
MRS. BENNET

LADY LUCAS
Musical Numbers: "I'll Regret It"—"Not Like Me"

SCENE 9

Longbourn Interior
MRS. BENNET
MR. BENNET
LYDIA
KITTY
MARY
ELIZABETH
COLLINS
JANE
Musical Numbers: "No"—"Mother Reprise"

ACT TWO

SCENE 1

Church Exterior
MRS. BENNET
LADY LUCAS
ELIZABETH
CHARLOTTE
COLLINS
Musical Numbers: "Wedding Talk"—"Wedding Talk Reprise"

SCENE 2

Rosings
COLLINS
MRS. BENNET
ELIZABETH
LADY CATHERINE
DARCY
BUTLER (Roos)
ANNE LUCAS (Mathis)
Musical Numbers: "Heart Has Won the Game"—"Goodby"—
"Love Will Find Way Repraise"—"A House In Town"

SCENE 3

Street
LYDIA
WICKHAM
JANE
Musical Number: "So This Is How It Is"

SCENE 4

Alehouse
DARCY
BINGLEY

LYDIA
WICKHAM
INNKEEPER ROSSI & (man)—Damon
2 WRESTLERS (Fleming, Sisco)
2 DRUNKEN OFFICERS { STERN
                        FREDERICKS
Musical Number: "Shropshire Whim"

SCENE 5

Longbourn Exterior

MRS. BENNET
ELIZABETH
JANE
DARCY
Musical Number: "Double Soliloquy"

SCENE 6

Longbourn Interior

MRS. BENNET
MARY
KITTY
JANE
CHARLOTTE
COLLINS
MR. BENNET
ELIZABETH
LADY CATHERINE
MAID (Welch)

SCENE 7

Longbourn Exterior

LYDIA
MARY
MRS. BENNET
MR. BENNET
ELIZABETH
WICKHAM
KITTY
JANE
Musical Number: "Fetch Carriage"

SCENE 8

Garden at Netherfield

DARCY
JANE
BINGLEY

MISS BINGLEY
ELIZABETH
WICKHAM
LYDIA
MARY
SOLDIER (Carter)
MRS. BENNET
MR. BENNET
KITTY
OFFICER (Hodes)
LADY LUCAS

First Impressions

ACT ONE

SCENE 1

Living room at Longbourn, a typical middle class English country home. The year is 1813. MARY, *the plain sister, is at her harp.* MR. BENNET *is doing his best to read and ignore the frightful sounds coming from the instrument.* JANE, KITTY *and* LYDIA *are seated Stage Left, occupied with sewing, etc. On rise,* MARY *is playing an introduction to a song. She finally starts singing. The song is "THERE'S A BLUEBIRD IN THE MEADOW." If* MARY *does not know this song another song of the period may be substituted. After two phrases ending with "meadow,"* LYDIA *speaks.*

LYDIA. (*Enters* U. C. *on second "Meadow," crosses* L. *to chair.*) Mary, please!

MR. BENNET. (*Calling Offstage.*) Mrs. Bennet! Mrs. Bennet!

MRS. BENNET. (*Entering from* U. L. *Crosses* R. *to* MARY, *then to* MR. BENNET.) Very nice. That will do, my dear.

MARY. (*Goes to* MRS. BENNET.) But, Mother, I've only just begun.

MRS. BENNET. And you've begun beautifully. Now stop. (MARY *tries to speak.*) Remember, all work and no play—

MARY. But, Mother, I *was* playing.

MRS. BENNET. Don't contradict Mother, dear.

MUSIC CUE: 3

(MARY *goes off* R.)

JANE. (*Rises and crosses to* MOTHER.) Look Mama, I've started a new shawl.

MRS. BENNET. That's nice, Jane dear. Where's Elizabeth?

JANE. She's out in the garden, talking. (*Crosses* U. C., *sits chair* L. *below window.*)

MRS. BENNET. Talking?

JANE. Yes.

LYDIA. (*Putting down pad and pen; reaches for cards.*) I think I'll play some piquet. (*Calls.*) Kitty—Kitty— Mother, may we play some piquet? (*Crosses* R. *to* MRS. BENNET.)

KITTY. (*Enters* R. 1, *with lace; crosses* C.) What is it, Lydia?

LYDIA. Shall we play some piquet? Mother, may we play some piquet?

KITTY. (*Crosses to* MOTHER.) Mama, this stitch is giving me a good deal of trouble. (*Gives* MOTHER *lace.*)

MRS. BENNET. Yes, dear, I'll see to it. Why don't you go and play piquet? (*Crosses* L. *to chair, sits.*) Oh, dear.

(*She sings "FIVE DAUGHTERS."*)

MUSIC: 4

MRS. BENNET.
> Five daughters
> How did it happen?
> How could I have managed
> To produce five of a kind?
>
> Five treasures
> Petticoated treasures
> If I see another stitch of lace
> I'll lose my mind (*Lace down.*)
>
> I don't deny (*Rises, crosses* D. R.)
> That my girls are precious pearls
> It's not that I'm not proud of them
> It's just there's such a crowd of them.
>
> Five problems (*Crosses* D. L.)
> Unmarried problems
> Maiden after maiden that's the way
> This family runs
> Maiden after maiden . . .
> Why didn't we have sons?
>
> Dear Mr. Bennet (*Crosses* R. *to* MR. BENNET.)
> He's a bit of a fraud
> He promised me diamonds
> And travel abroad
>
> He promised me riches
> And heaven knows what
> That's what I wanted
> Look what I got
>
> For years and years
> Prayed for a son
> But oh! How frustrating this is
> We've tried and tried and tried and tried
> Five tries
> Five misses

Oh! What a group (*Crosses* D. L.)
How they shout and run about
They'll hatch no proper plan that way
They'll never catch a man that way

Five maidens
Waiting to be mated
Jane's too shy, too easily hurt
Lydia's just a frivolous flirt
Kitty's always tagging along
Mary sings that horrible song
Lizzie
And Lizzie . . .

Dear Lord (*Spoken.*)
We need extra help with Lizzie . . .
So much needs to be done
And if you possibly can
Please keep her mouth closed.
Thank you.

(*Sung.*)
Daughters help a home to thrive
And I've got
Five!

(*Crosses* D. L. *on applause then* U. R. *to* MR. BENNET. *After song,*
MARGARET, *the maid, enters* R. 1, *carrying a letter.*)

MARGARET. (*Crosses to* MRS. BENNET.) This note just came,
ma'm.

MRS. BENNET. (*Taking note.*) Thank you, Margaret. (MAR-
GARET *goes.* MRS. BENNET *opens letter, reads for a moment;
crosses* D. L. *Excited.*) Oh, my goodness! How wonderful! (*Calling. The* FOUR GIRLS *gather around her.*)

MR. BENNET. What is it?

MRS. BENNET. Girls, the great house at Netherfield has been
taken, at last.

JANE. Who has taken it? (*Crosses* D. L.)

MRS. BENNET. Mr. Bennet, see what my sister says, right there.

MR. BENNET. (*Reading.*) "Netherfield Park, which is only a
mile from you, has just been taken over for one year by Mr.
Charles Bingley, a rich, single young man. This should be a
splendid thing for one of your daughters." (*He looks up.*) What
does she mean by that?

MRS. BENNET. She means he might marry one of them.

ELIZABETH. (*Entering* U. C., *crosses* D. C. *to* MRS. BENNET.)
Who's getting married?

MR. BENNET. Elizabeth, a rich, single young man named Bingley is moving into Netherfield Park.

ELIZABETH. Oh. And, Mama, you are setting our caps for him.

MRS. BENNET. What's wrong with that?

ELIZABETH. (*Crosses* L. *front sofa.*) But he may not care for any of us. Or, what is more important, even though he is rich and single, we may not care for him.

MRS. BENNET. (*Crosses* L. *to* ELIZABETH.) Elizabeth, sometimes your ideas are frightening. (ELIZABETH *sits sofa.*) Mr. Bennet, (*Crosses* R. *to* MR. BENNET) you must call at Netherfield immediately.

MR. BENNET. Why?

MRS. BENNET. To meet this young man and invite him here.

MR. BENNET. (*Rises.*) I see no occasion for that. You and the girls may go. Or perhaps you can send them by themselves. It might be safer if you stayed away. You are as handsome as any of them. This rich single young gentleman might like you best of all.

MRS. BENNET. You flatter me. But when a woman has five grown daughters, it's time she gave up thinking of her own beauty. No, you must go.

ELIZABETH. Shouldn't we give Mr. Bingley a chance to unpack his things?

MR. BENNET. (*He sits.*) Yes. I fail to see the need for all this hurry.

MRS. BENNET. Mr. Bennet, do you never think of your daughters' futures? Do you realize what will happen when you die?

MR. BENNET. Yes. I am planning to go to Heaven.

MRS. BENNET. There you go thinking of yourself again. Not caring that your daughters will be destitute because you are leaving everything to that cousin of yours. That—that odious Mr. Collins.

MR. BENNET. (*Rises.*) Is it really impossible for you to grasp the fact that the law of entail is not of my devising? This estate was entailed when I inherited it. It must, by law, go to a male heir—and that is my cousin, Mr. Collins. By the way, I've had a letter from him— (*He reaches in his pocket.*)

MRS. BENNET. I am not interested in Mr. Collins. If you choose to leave him everything—that is your privilege. I have to think of my children. My wretched, husbandless children.

(MR. BENNET *sits.*)

ELIZABETH. Mama, I don't think of us as wretched and husbandless.

MRS. BENNET. (*Crosses* D. R.) Well, I do.

JANE. Lizzie, we are husbandless.

LYDIA. (*Crosses* U. R. *to* C. *between* MR. BENNET *and sofa.*) And I'm wretched. I'm past sixteen. If I don't marry soon, I shall die. I shall really die.

MRS. BENNET. Now that is sound thinking. (*She exits* R.)

ELIZABETH. Well, Papa—

MR. BENNET. Well, I guess, I'll go call on Mr. Bingley. (*He starts off* R.)

ELIZBETH. Good luck.

KITTY. (*Crosses* R. *to sofa; gets lace, crosses* L. *to chair.*) Papa, don't forget to invite him to the Assembly next week.

MR. BENNET. Yes, dear. (*He exits* R.)

MARY. I wonder if Mr. Bingley is musical.

LYDIA. I don't care about any old Mr. Bingley. I just hope the Assembly has lots and lots of officers from the Regiment.

KITTY. (*Crosses* U. R. *behind sofa to* LYDIA.) So do I. What will you wear, Lydia?

LYDIA. Well, I—

ELIZABETH. (*She has been listening. Now she interrupts.*) You know, we really are wretched, husbandless creatures, just as our mother says. Well, I don't care if I ever marry or not.

(GIRLS *look stunned.*)

JANE. (*Crosses* L. *front of sofa and to chair.*) But, Lizzie, girls are supposed to marry.

ELIZABETH. Why?

MARY. (*Crosses* D. C.) It's the thing to do.

ELIZABETH. And therefore you're planning all sorts of ways to make yourselves pleasing to men you don't care about. Well, I don't like to do the things that are things to do.

JANE. Lizzie, please.

LYDIA. If Mama ever heard you.

MUSIC: 5

(ELIZABETH *sings "I'M ME."*)

ELIZABETH.
    Is what I'm saying treasonable?
               (MARY *drifts* L. *to desk.*)
SISTERS.
    Guilty
    Guilty (GIRLS *sit.*)
ELIZABETH.
    Am I so unreasonable?
SISTERS.
    Guilty
    Guilty

ELIZABETH.
    Am I the nemesis
    About the family premises?

SISTERS.
    Guilty
    Guilty

ELIZABETH.
    Well, if that's the way I am
    That's the way I am

    I believe in saying what I think
    And I know no other way to be
    I am not the dainty feminine kind
    Ladylike and overrefined
    I just can't help speaking my mind
    I'm me
    I'm me
    Just me

    I believe in doing what I like
    Though at times the world may disagree
    I've been told I ought to try to give in
    But I don't know how to begin
    Much to everybody's chagrin
    I'm me
    I'm me

    Why should I care (*Crosses* D. L.)
    If I'm not a maiden fair
    If, alas, I'm not the lass with the delicate air (*Crosses* D. R.)

    Should I care?
    Should I care?

    I refuse to bow before the wind
    Like the fragile branches of a tree
    I suppose I'm just an obstinate fool
    One part woman, the other part mule
    Try to make me anything else, you'll see
    I will never change
    I'm me.

        (MUSIC *under dialogue after first chorus.*)

  MARY. Lizzie, I'm afraid your attitude will always make things very difficult for you.

  LYDIA. You might as well not even go to the Assemblies.

  KITTY. (*Rises.*) You just keep offending more and more men.

(ELIZABETH *looks at* JANE.)

JANE. I'm afraid they're right, Lizzie. (*Rises.*)

(MUSIC *swells and dims.*)

LYDIA. (*Stepping up to* ELIZABETH.) Miss Bennet, may I have this dance?

ELIZABETH. I'm sorry, sir, but my feet have not yet recovered from our last dance. (LYDIA *crosses back to sofa.*)

KITTY. Miss Bennet, shall we sit down and have a talk? (*Crosses* C. *to her.*)

ELIZABETH. Certainly, sir. But this time I would like to do some of the talking. (KITTY *crosses back.*)

JANE. Lizzie, I remember when you said that. He left town.

(ELIZABETH *into last section of song.*)

ELIZABETH.
    And I'm glad he did.

(*Crosses* L. *to each girl* JANE, LYDIA, MARY, KITTY. *They sit one by one as* ELIZABETH *comes to them.*)

    Why should I care
    If I'm not a maiden fair
    If, Alas, I'm not the lass with the delicate air . . .

    Should I care?
    Should I care?

I refuse to bow before the wind	GIRLS.
Like the fragile branches of a tree	Lizzie!
I suppose I'm just an obstinate fool	Lizzie!
One part woman, the other part mule.	What an exas-
Try to make me anything else, you'll see	perating girl.

GIRLS.
    It's hopeless
    So hopeless
ELIZABETH.
    I will never change
    I'm me.
SISTERS.
    You're you.
ELIZABETH.
    I will never change.
    I'm me. (*Sits.*)

CLOSE IN

ACT ONE

SCENE 2

A road in Meryton. TRAVELER *is a high box hedge with a drop behind it.* MR. BENNET *enters* L. *carrying a pair of clipping shears. He is dressed in his old gardening clothes.* MRS. BENNET *enters from* R., *all dressed up, carrying a hat box. She stops as she sees* MR. BENNET.

MRS. BENNET. (*Enters* R. *1, crosses to* MR. BENNET.) Mr. Bennet, please do go home and put on some decent clothes.

MR. BENNET. (*Pointing to shears.*) I was on my way to have these sharpened. I have to do our hedge.

MRS. BENNET. Oh, who cares about that silly hedge? When you die, it's going to go to your cousin Collins, anyway. You shouldn't go around looking like that. Mr. Bingley might arrive today and drive by and see you.

MR. BENNET. There's no reason to think he's arriving today. When I called at Netherfield, they said they didn't know when he was arriving. (LADY LUCAS *and* CHARLOTTE *enter from* R.) Oh, look! It's Lady Lucas and her daughter.

MRS. BENNET. Oh, calamity! (*She goes to them, embraces them.*) Oh, how nice. I've been pining to see you.

MR. BENNET. Charlotte, how are you?

LADY LUCAS. We can only stop for a minute. I just had to tell you the news. Mr. Bingley is arriving today.

(MRS. BENNET *hands* MR. BENNET *her hat box.*)

MR. BENNET. I'll go and change my clothes. (*He exits* L. *with hat box.*)

LADY LUCAS. We are on our way to Meryton. Charlotte is being fitted with a new taffeta.

MRS. BENNET. Dressing up for Mr. Bingley, eh?

CHARLOTTE. It won't be any use. The moment he sets eyes on your daughters we will all be out of the running.

LADY LUCAS. You are much too modest, my dear.

MRS. BENNET. But sensible.

LADY LUCAS. You may not have beauty, but you have character. And some men prefer it.

CHARLOTTE. *Some men.* (*Exits* L. *1.*)

MRS. BENNET. When is Mr. Bingley coming?

LADY LUCAS. I'm not certain, but it's today. And let me tell you something else. He's not coming alone.

MRS. BENNET. Who's he bringing. A fiancee? A mistress?

LADY LUCAS. No, no, no! He's bringing two people. One is his sister.

MRS. BENNET. I don't like sisters. (*Crosses* D. L.) But, still— (*Crosses* R. *to her.*) if he must have one, it's best to have her where I can watch her. Who is the other person?

LADY LUCAS. Ah.

MRS. BENNET. Ah?

LADY LUCAS. Prepare yourself. Another bachelor. Even richer than Mr. Bingley.

MRS. BENNET. Heavens, twice blessed. What's his name?

LADY LUCAS. He is a Mr. Fitzwilliam Darcy, of Pemberly. And I was asked not to repeat this.

MRS. BENNET. So?

LADY LUCAS. So they tell me his income runs to five thousand a year.

(MRS. BENNET *registers shock.* LADY LUCAS *goes into song,* "*HAVE YOU HEARD THE NEWS?*")

MUSIC: 7

LADY LUCAS.
    Five thousand pounds a year
    Is making its way from London to here
    Making its way from London to here
    Five thousand pounds a year. (*Crosses* L.)
MRS. BENNET.
    You mustn't repeat a word of this
    I'm sworn to secrecy.
    You mustn't repeat a word.
    But just between you and me

    Have you heard the news? The news?
    Extraordinary news.
    An unmarried gentleman's coming here
    With an annual income of six thousand a year.
CHORUS.
    Six
    Six thousand pounds a year
    is making its way from London to here.
    Finding its way from London to here.
    Six thousand pounds a year.
MRS. BENNET.
    Have you heard the news? The news?
    Extraordinary news?
    A member of Parliament's coming here.
    With an annual income of eight thousand a year.
CHORUS.
    Eight

Eight thousand pounds a year
Is making its way from London to here.

MRS. BENNET.

Trotting its way from London to here

CHORUS.

Eight thousand pounds a year.

MRS. BENNET.

You mustn't repeat a word of this
I'm sworn to secrecy
You mustn't repeat a word
But just between you and me,

Have you heard the news? The news?
Extraordinary news.
The son of a baron is coming here
With an annual income of ten thousand a year.

CHORUS.

Ten.
Ten thousand pounds a year
Is making its way from London to here.
Rushing its way from London to here.

MRS. BENNET.

Twelve thousand pounds

LADY LUCAS.

Five

CHORUS.

Twelve thousand pounds a year.

GIRLS.	MEN.
You mustn't repeat a word of this.	Have you heard
I'm sworn to secrecy	The news? The news?
You mustn't repeat a word but	Extraordinary news.
	An unmarried gentleman's coming here.
Just between you and me	
He's got twelve thousand a year.	With an annual income of twelve thousand a year.

CHORUS.

News?
Extraordinary news, extraordinary news.
Extraordinary news, extraordinary news.

Twelve thousand pounds a year is making its way from London to here
Twelve thousand pounds a year is making its way from London to here
An unmarried gentleman
A member of Parliament

The son of a baron
The Prince Regent's cousin

Welcome, welcome.
Welcome to Hertfordshire.
DARCY.
Onward—
MRS. BENNET. (*Dialogue.*) Utterly charming.
CHORUS.
Welcome, welcome,
Welcome.

(*Right before end of song, we see tops of horses' heads Upstage of the hedge. They move across Stage and moving with them we see the heads and shoulders of* MR. BINGLEY, MISS BINGLEY *and* DARCY. *As they come Center Stage, the carriage stops. The* CROWD *looks up at them in awe, then as if he didn't care for what he sees,* DARCY *signals for the carriage to proceed.*)

DARCY. (*To* COACHMAN.) Onward!

(*They exit* R., *as the* LOCALS *finish the song.*)
                 MUSIC: 8

ACT ONE

SCENE 3

Assembly in Meryton. Full stage. Polka-mazurka is in progress. KITTY *and* ELIZABETH *are dancing.* LYDIA *and* WICKHAM *are dancing* D. S.

END DANCE MUSIC TO: 8A
(MAZURKA)

LYDIA. Don't you think we dance beautifully together, Captain Wickham?
WICKHAM. I suspect you dance beautifully with anyone, Miss Lydia. I know I do. (*He spots* ELIZABETH.) Tell me, who is that lovely creature?
LYDIA. That lovely creature is my sister Elizabeth. How can you bear to look at anyone else when you're dancing with me?
WICKHAM. A soldier must learn to bear many things. I'd like to be presented to her.
LYDIA. (*In a bit of a pique, she promptly dances toward* ELIZABETH, *continues to speak as she dances.*) Lizzie, this is Captain

Wickham. He wants to meet you. He thinks you're a lovely creature.

(WICKHAM *and* ELIZABETH *bow to each other as they dance.*)

WICKHAM. (*To* LYDIA.) Some day I'll tell you what kind of creature you are. (LYDIA *dances away with another* OFFICER. ELIZABETH *dances now with* WICKHAM.) After that introduction I hardly know how to begin, Miss Elizabeth. Perhaps I should start with a witty remark about the weather.

ELIZABETH. Could you make such a remark fit for a young lady's ears?

WICKHAM. Perhaps the weather is too dangerous a subject.

ELIZABETH. To be quite safe I shall ask you how you like being stationed in Hartfordshire.

WICKHAM. Ah, that's not a safe question. I'm just discovering that I like it prodigiously. Miss Elizabeth, I hope you will ask me when I began to like Hartfordshire so prodigiously.

ELIZABETH. I will. When did you?

WICKHAM. The moment I saw you.

ELIZABETH. You officers talk as prettily as you look.

WICKHAM. Thank you. You know, your sister warned me that if I made any pretty speeches to you, you were likely to cut my head off.

ELIZABETH. My whole family thinks I'm rude. I suppose I am. Well, I just say what I think. And with most men that turns out to be rude.

(*DANCE now picks up again, comes to a vigorous end, leaving* DANCERS *breathless.*)

WICKHAM. Your family doesn't appreciate you. I think you are quite charming.

ELIZABETH. Oh, I'm just on my best behavior tonight. After all, we are going to have the honor of meeting the magnificent Mr. Bingley and the noble Mr. Darcy.

WICKHAM. (*Reacting.*) Did you say—Darcy?

ELIZABETH. Yes. Mr. Bingley's friend. Do you know him?

MUSIC: 8B

(*MUSIC starts for POLKA ENCORE.* WICKHAM *takes* ELIZA-BETH'S *arm to dance. They start dancing, cross to* L. *and return.* ELIZABETH *ends cross near* MRS. BENNET, *seated Stage* R. *Suddenly the dance seems to slow down.* MISS BINGLEY, MR. BINGLEY, *and* DARCY *enter the ballroom* D. L. *The* THREE *them stand there, looking at the people.* KITTY *and* LYDIA *go to their* MOTHER. JANE *is standing back of her chair. They stare at the new arrivals.* LADY LUCAS *hurries from* U. L. *with* SIR WILLIAM. *They go to the three new* GUESTS.)

BUTLER. (*Has brought in guests. Begins announcement.*) Ladies and gentlemen. (*MUSIC and dancing stop.*) Miss Bingley, Mr. Bingley and Mr. Darcy.

(*As their names are announced,* MISS BINGLEY *and* MR. BINGLEY *enter. After a pause,* DARCY *enters.* BUTLER *clears* L. PEOPLE *bow.*)

WICKHAM. (*To* ELIZABETH.) Will you excuse me? (*He goes off* R., *leaving* ELIZABETH *looking puzzled.*)

LADY LUCAS. This is indeed an honor.

(*There are polite greetings from the* THREE. ELIZABETH *joins her mother and sisters* R. *Conversational focus now goes there. Cue for string quartet.*)

MUSIC: 8C

MRS. BENNET. Very distinguished, very distinguished. Kitty— Kitty, your dress is too decollete. Pull it up a little. (KITTY *does so.*) Lydia, there is perspiration on your nose. Don't get so hot. It's very unladylike. And, Jane—

JANE. Yes, Mama.

MRS. BENNET. Of course, you're quite perfect, my dear. Lizzie! Lizzie! (ELIZABETH *turns to her.*) Lizzie, do try to make a good impression. You can be so appealing when you want to be. Oh, Mary— (MARY *turns.*) Try to sparkle a little. Just a little. (MARY *puts on a bright smile.*)

DARCY. Well, I think we've been here long enough.

BINGLEY. Now, Darcy, I think it all looks very pleasant. We'll have a good time.

DARCY. Bingley, you are too easily satisfied. I see nothing but a lot of provincials being very provincial.

(BINGLEY *moves* U. L. *with* LADY LUCAS *and* SIR WILLIAM.)

MRS. BENNET. Isn't Mr. Darcy a handsome man?

ELIZABETH. And doesn't he know it!

JANE. I like Mr. Bingley better. Mr. Darcy's so— (*She can't find word.*)

ELIZABETH. I know what you mean. If his nose were any higher in the air, it would cut off his vision.

MRS. BENNET. Girls, you shouldn't judge people before you've met them, especially not rich, single, handsome young men. It's un-christian.

JANE. Well, I still like Mr. Bingley better.

ELIZABETH. And he likes you, too.

JANE. Me? Why, he hasn't noticed me. (*Flustered.*)

ELIZABETH. He's been staring at you as though he were a pointer and you were a grouse.

JANE. (*Turning away.*) Lizzie, please.

BINGLEY. (*To* SIR WILLIAM.) Sir William— (SIR WILLIAM *comes to* BINGLEY *from* U. L.) tell me, who is that uncommonly handsome girl?

LADY LUCAS. (*Leaping in.*) That's my daughter, Charlotte. Surely you remember.

BINGLEY. (*Pointing.*) No, I mean the one in pink.

SIR WILLIAM. Uh—uh, that's one of the Bennet girls.

LADY LUCAS. (*Disgusted.*) There are thousands of them. (*She walks away.*)

BINGLEY. (*To* SIR WILLIAM.) Will you present me?

SIR WILLIAM. Delighted. (*They cross towards the* BENNET *party.*)

ELIZABETH. What did I tell you?

MRS. BENNET. Oh! They're coming this way. Kitty, your dress. Mary, sparkle.

SIR WILLIAM. Oh, Mrs. Bennet, uh—uh, may I present Mr. Bingley. Mrs. Bennet, Miss Elizabeth Bennet, Miss Jane Bennet—

MRS. BENNET. (*Leaping in.*) Mr. Bingley, we're all so delighted that you've taken Netherfield. Having that great house stand empty was a loss to the whole community. Like an oyster shell without an oyster in it. And now, at last, it has its oyster—you.

BINGLEY. Well, I may be the oyster, Madam. But if I may be permitted to say so, it is you who have the pearl.

MRS. BENNET. (*Throwing a convulsion.*) Oh God! That's witty! Girls, did you hear that? Please say it again, Mr. Bingley.

BINGLEY. Well, I—

(JANE *crosses* D. R. *of post into view.*)

MRS. BENNET. (*Going right on.*) Jane, say something to Mr. Bingley.

JANE. Good evening, sir.

BINGLEY. May I have the honor of this dance, Miss Bennet?

MUSIC: 9

JANE. With pleasure. (JANE *and* BINGLEY *go to join waltz.* MRS. BENNET *rises, exits* R. *with* LADY LUCAS.)

CHARLOTTE. Lizzy. (*Crosses* D. R.)

ELIZABETH. Hello, Charlotte.

CHARLOTTE. You and I shall sit this one out together. Oh, why is England cursed with so many more women than men?

ELIZABETH. I think it's the climate. Men don't seem to flourish in damp air. Come, let's find the wallflowers' nook.

CHARLOTTE. Lizzy, do you think Miss Bingley is engaged to Mr. Darcy?

ELIZABETH. If she is, she ought to break it. No man could be in love and look like that. (*They stroll out* D. R., *reappear* D. L. *They take seats Upstage, nearly out of sight.*)

MISS BINGLEY. Really, Mr. Darcy. Did you ever see such people? I don't know why we came here.

DARCY. Nor do I. However, your brother seems to be getting along famously.

MISS BINGLEY. He has a vulgar gift for enjoying himself. I wish he were more like you. You know, Mr. Darcy, I've never seen you enjoy yourself. I admire that.

DARCY. Thank you.

BINGLEY. You know, Miss Bennet, you have done a very extraordinary thing.

JANE. What?

BINGLEY. You have talked to me about all your friends in Hertfordshire without saying one malicious word. That's very rare in a young lady.

JANE. Oh, but my friends here are all such agreeable people.

BINGLEY. How could anyone help being agreeable to you? (LADY LUCAS *has joined* MRS. BENNET *and is watching the dancing. MUSIC stops. The other* DANCERS *stop dancing.* JANE *and* BINGLEY *keep on dancing, not realizing the dance is over.* MISS BINGLEY *and* DARCY *go to them. They stand there and watch them. To* JANE.) Isn't that delightful? That you like riding as much as I do.

JANE. Delightful.

BINGLEY. I hope we may be able to ride together sometime.

JANE. That would be nice. (*They become aware of the presence of the* OTHERS, *and the fact that the dance is over.*)

BINGLEY. (*Flustered.*) Oh, I didn't know the music had stopped.

DARCY. You seemed to be making your own.

BINGLEY. Caroline, this is Miss Bennet. My sister, Miss Bingley, and Mr. Darcy.

MISS BINGLEY. Miss Bennet, will you take a little stroll about the room with me?

JANE. With pleasure. (BINGLEY *moves to accompany them.*)

MISS BINGLEY. Oh, no, Charles. You were not invited. I have a thousand things I want to ask Miss Bennet. (BINGLEY *exits* L.) You must come over to Netherfield one day. I shall be so bored.

JANE. Bored?

MISS BINGLEY. Oh, you know—marooned out here in the wilderness.

JANE. Oh, yes—

MISS BINGLEY. We'll arrange it, shall we—?

JANE. That would be delightful.

MISS BINGLEY. Very soon? (*They stroll out of sight* U. L. MRS. BENNET *rises.*)

LADY LUCAS. Think of gaining a son and losing a daughter. (MRS. BENNET *exits* R. *with* LADY LUCAS.)

DARCY. (*Crosses* D. L. *to* BINGLEY.) Don't you think we should be leaving soon?

BINGLEY. We've just arrived! I intend to stay and do lots and lots of dancing. Why don't you go and find someone and dance?

DARCY. Dance? With whom? Your sister is occupied, and there isn't another woman in the room that it wouldn't be a punishment for me to stand up with.

BINGLEY. But the place is full of pretty girls.

DARCY. I've noticed only one, and I'm sure if I asked her to dance, you'd have my head.

BINGLEY. Naturally—but there's that sister of hers, the one that was standing next to her, Miss Elizabeth. They say she has quite a lively wit.

DARCY. A provincial young lady with a lively wit. I'm sure she has sparkling conversations with her cow.

BINGLEY. I think she's charming.

DARCY. Well, she looks tolerable enough—but I'm in no humor tonight to give consequence to the middle class at play.

(DARCY *and* BINGLEY *leave the room, and* ELIZABETH *and* CHARLOTTE *appear.* ELIZABETH *is furious.*)

ELIZABETH. (*Rises, crosses* D. L.) What a charming man! Of all the arrogant, detestable snobs.

CHARLOTTE. Oh, but Lizzy—he didn't know you were listening.

ELIZABETH. What difference does that make—he'd have said it just the same if he had. (*Then carricaturing him.*) "Well, she looks tolerable enough, but I'm in no humor tonight to give consequence to the middle class at play." I'd like to wring his noble neck!

(MR. STUBBS, *an old man, bows in* CHARLOTTE's *direction.*)

MUSIC: 10

CHARLOTTE. Lizzie, I must go. I have this dance with old Mr. Stubbs. He's never learned the steps, but he likes the exercise and it gets me away from the wall.

(DARCY *crosses* U. C., *caught by* BINGLEY, *who brings him* D. L. *to* ELIZABETH.)

BINGLEY. Miss Bennet, may I present Mr. Darcy. He is most eager to invite you to dance. (*Crosses* U .C.)

DARCY. (*Annoyed by the introduction, but polite.*) Now that you have been forewarned of my eagerness to dance with you, I hope you will do me the honor.

ELIZABETH. (*Seated* L. *Stunned, then gathering herself.*) Mr. Darcy, I am afraid the honor of dancing with you is more than I can bear. Please excuse me. (*Turning away from him.*)

DARCY. (*Shocked.*) Am—am I to understand that you do not wish to dance with me, Miss Bennet?

ELIZABETH. Well, let's put it this way—no!

DARCY. (*Attempting to recover.*) The loss is mine, I'm sure.

ELIZABETH. You would be the best judge of that. (DARCY *bows and is about to leave.* WICKHAM *enters from* D. S. R. ELIZABETH *sees him. Rises.*) Captain Wickham.

WICKHAM. (*Crosses* D. L., *towards* ELIZABETH.) Miss Elizabeth, if you're not engaged, will you honor me with the next dance?

ELIZABETH. I should be very happy to dance with you. Oh, this is Captain Wickham, Mr. Darcy.

WICKHAM. (*Cautiously.*) Mr. Darcy and I have met before.

DARCY. (*Cutting him dead.*) We have indeed. (*He crosses to* D. R., *stands.*)

ELIZABETH. The man must be mad—to act that way towards a gentleman such as yourself.

WICKHAM. (*Cutting in sharply after the word "gentleman."*) Miss Bennet, I have known him for many years. My father was once steward of the Darcy estates at Pemberley. Mr. Darcy and I grew up together.

ELIZABETH. But he considered you beneath him.

WICKHAM. He has never considered me a gentleman. In his opinion, I lack—well, I mustn't trust myself on that subject.

ELIZABETH. I'll tell you what you lack, Captain Wickham. You lack arrogance, bad manners, insolence and all the other admirable qualities with which Mr. Darcy is so splendidly endowed. (*She rises.*)

(WICKHAM *bows and they join the dance.* DARCY *and* ELIZABETH *look at each other. Then they start "A PERFECT EVENING."*)

MUSIC: 11

DARCY.

    I've seen her kind before
    With the look in her eye
    And the vulgar laugh
    And the uppity air
    Of true riffraff
    It's exceedingly plain to see
    She's everything you'd think she'd be

ELIZABETH. (L. C. *with* WICKHAM. WICKHAM *dances around her.*)

    I've seen his kind before
    With his head in the clouds
    And his nose in the air
    And a shirt that's stuffed
    From here to there

It's exceedingly plain to see
He's everything I thought he'd be

Proud, proud, proud, proud
He's abominably proud
He's abominably proud

DARCY.
Talk, talk, talk, talk
She's unconsciously loud
She's unconsciously loud.

ELIZABETH.
Vain, vain, vain, vain
He's incorrigibly vain
He's incorrigibly vain

DARCY.
Common, common,
Common, common
She's unusually plain
Most unusually plain.

(DARCY *starts* L., *finds himself dancing. As the dance progresses and partners change,* DARCY *and* ELIZABETH *find themselves dancing with each other, which leads us into the duet chorus of the song. This duet is preceded by dialogue, as follows.*)

DARCY. It seems you have to put up with me, after all.

ELIZABETH. Well, it's only for a short time.

DARCY. I'm still somewhat puzzled by your attitude.

ELIZABETH. Mr. Darcy, if we must converse, let's stay on the aristocratic level. Small talk.

DARCY. Small talk? I'm not very good at it.

ELIZABETH. I think a bit of chitchat may keep us from being conspicuous—and make this dance more bearable. Shall we try it?

DARCY. If you like. (*Into balance of number.*)

ELIZABETH.
A perfect evening.

DARCY.
Ah! Yes.

ELIZABETH.
A splendid night.

DARCY.
Indeed.

ELIZABETH.
We're all impressed with
Your superb
Reputation.

DARCY.
A perfect evening

    A pure delight
    Such friendly faces
    And polite
    Conversation

    My reception
    Has certainly been complete.

ELIZABETH.
    And why not, sir?
    You've swept us off our feet.

ELIZABETH *and* DARCY.
    The sound of music
    A fetching tune
    How very pleasant
    Everything
    Seems so fit and right
    Tonight
    Is a perfectly perfect night.

ORCHESTRATION.
    A perfect evening
    A lovely night
    We're all imp—

ELIZABETH.
    Proud, proud.

DARCY.
    Common, common.

ELIZABETH.
    Vain, vain.

DARCY.
    Talk, talk, talk.

ELIZABETH.
    Nose in the air.

DARCY.
    Vulgar laugh.

ELIZABETH.
    Stuffed shirt.

DARCY.
    True riffraff.

ELIZABETH.
    Proper.

DARCY.
    Pretty.

ELIZABETH.
    Handsome.

DARCY.
    Different.

ELIZABETH.
    Vain.

DARCY.
　　Common.
ELIZABETH.
　　Proud.
ELIZABETH *and* DARCY.
　　Impossible!
　　Oh!

　　A perfect evening
　　A pure delight.
DARCY.
　　Can I be dreaming?
ELIZABETH.
　　Everything
　　Seems so fit and right
　　Tonight
　　Is a perfectly perfect night.
BOTH.
　　Impossible!

ACT ONE

SCENE 4

A few days later.

MUSIC: 12

Exterior Longbourn, in One. MR. BENNET *at Stage* R., *trimming his hedge.* MRS. BENNET *enters* C. *hurriedly.*

MRS. BENNET. (*Enters* C., *crosses* R. *to* MR. BENNET.) Oh, Mr. Bennet, would you please have the carriage brought around?

MR. BENNET. The carriage? Are you going out, my dear?

MRS. BENNET. Your voice seems to have such a hopeful ring. No, I'm not going out. The carriage is for Jane.

MR. BENNET. For Jane? (*He looks puzzled.*)

MRS. BENNET. Jane is going to Netherfield today. She has been invited to have dinner with Mr. Bingley and his sister. You were told about it. Sometimes I think that you are able to shut off your ears.

MR. BENNET. Not yet, my dear, but I'm practicing.

MRS. BENNET. This is a very important evening for Jane. Mr. Bingley is falling in love with her. I know it.

(KITTY, LYDIA, MARY *and* JANE *enter* C. *They are all fussing with* JANE's *cloak.*)

KITTY. You look lovely, Jane dear.

JANE. Thank you, Kitty. Papa, is the carriage ready?

MR. BENNET. Well, no, Jane dear, but it will be here in a few moments. (*Looking at* MRS. BENNET *a little nervously.*) I sent it over to Maryton to pick up my cousin.

MRS. BENNET. Your what?

MR. BENNET. My cousin, Mr. Collins. He's arriving on the afternoon coach.

MRS. BENNET. (*Stunned.*) Mr. Collins is coming here, to this house?

MR. BENNET. Only for a week or so.

MRS. BENNET. Why wasn't I told?

MR. BENNET. I have tried to tell you several times. Perhaps if you would let me explain why he's coming—

MRS. BENNET. Since he's going to inherit the estate when you are gone, he's probably coming to take your pulse. (*Crosses* D. R.) Dreadful man.

ELIZABETH. (*Entering* R. *1.*) Papa, the carriage is driving up. It must be Mr. Collins.

MR. BENNET. I had better go greet him. (*He exits* C.)

MRS. BENNET. (*To* ELIZABETH.) You knew he was coming? That horrid man.

ELIZABETH. Mother, you have never even met Mr. Collins.

MR. BENNET. (*Entering with* MR. COLLINS.) We are all out here, Mr. Collins.

(GIRLS *rise*, MRS. BENNET *groans quietly and turns away.*)

COLLINS. Ah, the beauty of all England seems to be assembled in your little garden.

MR. BENNET. Mrs. Bennet has been eager to know you.

(COLLINS *crosses* R. *to* MRS. BENNET.)

MRS. BENNET. MMmmm. How do you do, Mr. Collins? I trust your journey was not too fatiguing.

COLLINS. Dear madam, the fatigues of the journey have been melted away by the warmth of your gracious hospitality. And may I say—

MR. BENNET. (*Cutting in. Taking* COLLINS *by arm, crosses* L. C. *towards* GIRLS.) These are my daughters, Mr. Collins. This is Elizabeth.

COLLINS. Oh, this is indeed a privilege.

ELIZABETH. Thank you.

MR. BENNET. And Jane— Mary, Kitty and Lydia—our youngest.

COLLINS. Beauty, beauty. I am quite overpowered. I am absolutely devastated. Madam. (*Crosses* R. *to* MRS. BENNET.) I have heard much of the charm and beauty of your daughters. But in my humble opinion, their fame falls far short of reality. And may I say—

MRS. BENNET. (*Interrupting him.*) Mr. Collins, unfortunately beauty is not all that counts. Even beautiful girls must have money. (*Backing* COLLINS L. C. *of arch.*) And when one thinks that there are some people who think nothing of deliberately— (*To* MR. BENNET *and continuing on.*) disinheriting their daughters, and when one thinks that there are other people who think nothing of making other people destitute, it makes one think, doesn't it? (*She exits* C.)

COLLINS. (*Bewildered.*) Quite so. Quite so.

MR. BENNET. (*Leaping in.*) Mr. Collins, how is your patroness?

COLLINS. Very well, thank you.

MR. BENNET. (*Crosses* R. *to* ELIZABETH.) You know, Mr. Collins has a most distinguished patroness, Lady Catherine de Bourgh.

ELIZABETH. Lady who?

COLLINS. (*Shocked.*) Lady Catherine de Bourgh. Miss Elizabeth, surely you know her. Lady Catherine is a great noblewoman. Never in my life have I witnessed such behavior in a person of rank. Such grace, such condescension. I serve her in the very humble capacity of librarian and curator of her art treasures, and yet from time to time she speaks to me.

ELIZABETH. Really?

COLLINS. Yes. By the way, her nephew is, I believe, visiting in this vicinity. A gentleman named Darcy. A charming man. Of course, I doubt that you would meet him.

ELIZABETH. I have met him and I doubt that he is charming.

COLLINS. Oh, he is. Just like his aunt. She's a delightful person. (*Puts hat on.*) You know, Lady Catherine has promised me that when I marry, she will come to visit.

MRS. BENNET. (*Enters from* C. *hedge.*) Marry? Did you say when you marry? You're planning to marry?

COLLINS. Madam, that is the purpose of my visit here. I explained it in my letter to your husband.

MRS. BENNET. My husband never tells me anything. You tell me, Mr. Collins.

COLLINS. Well, madam, as you are aware, when a certain melancholy event occurs, (*Takes hat off.*) I shall be the involuntary means of disinheriting your daughters. I have long felt it my duty to make such reparation as was in my power.

MRS. BENNET. What else could a gentleman do?

COLLINS. Unfortunately, I cannot make amends to more than one. The difficulty now is one of choice. (*He looks at the* GIRLS, *steps* R. *to* ELIZABETH.)

ELIZABETH. (*Starting off.*) Mama, there are some new kittens in the stable. I want to see that they are looked after.

MRS. BENNET. (*She makes a gesture to stop her.*) Lizzie— (*Inaudible indication.*)

ELIZABETH. (*Crosses* L.) Really, those kittens need looking after.

MRS. BENNET. That is a problem for their mother.

ELIZABETH. Mama, I imagine Mr. Collins must want to rest after his long journey.

MRS. BENNET. He doesn't look tired to me.

(ELIZABETH *crosses* L. *to* SISTERS *on bench.*)

COLLINS. As a matter of fact, I am a bit tired. It was very considerate of Miss Elizabeth to think of me.

MR. BENNET. Come along, Mr. Collins. Let me take you in.

COLLINS. (*Crosses* C.) After you, Mr. Bennet. (BENNET *goes* C. COLLINS *starts to follow. He stops, turns.*) I should like to change from these travel clothes into something more fitting—to prepare myself for my difficult mission. (*He smirks at* ELIZABETH *and exits* C.)

MRS. BENNET. (*Crosses* L. *to* ELIZABETH.) What a charming man. Elizabeth, you were very rude to him.

ELIZABETH. (*Crosses* R. C.) Mama, I think Jane's carriage is ready.

MRS. BENNET. (*Crosses* L. *to* JANE.) Oh, yes. Now, Jane, this is a very important dinner for you. Don't forget what I told you. About Mr. Bingley—don't be too distant with him. And, Jane, try to sit where he can see you in profile. You know, dear, you have the loveliest profile in Hertfordshire. And, incidentally, (*Takes* JANE *Downstage.*) if he should suggest a stroll before dinner, don't refuse. There is lots of shrubbery around Netherfield. Delightfully secluded.

JANE. Yes, Mama.

(*There is a RUMBLE OF THUNDER Offstage.*)

ELIZABETH. (*Looks up.*) There won't be much strolling today, Mama.

MRS. BENNET. (*Looking up.*) Oh! (*Crosses* L. *to* JANE.) Dear me, Lizzie, I'm afraid you're right— It's going to rain. And I was counting so much on that shrubbery. (*Suddenly making up her mind.*) Lizzie— (*Crosses* R. *to her.*) go tell the boy we won't be using the carriage and have him saddle up the horse for Jane. (JANE *crosses* R., *listening.*)

ELIZABETH. A horse? But, Mama, you can't send Jane out on horseback. It is going to rain hard and she will catch cold.

MRS. BENNET. Nonsense. A few drops of water never hurt anyone. Besides, if it rains she won't be able to ride home after dinner. They'll have to keep her all night. There's nothing like wet weather for engagements. (ELIZABETH *goes off* R. *shaking her head.*)

JANE. But, Mama— (*Crosses* L., *sits on bench.*)

MRS. BENNET. Don't worry, darling. It was during a thunderstorm that your dear father and I became engaged. (JANE *sits on bench, hopelessly.*)

MUSIC: 13
(*Lead into song "AS LONG AS THERE'S A MOTHER."*)

MRS. BENNET.
> So hurry, Jane, hurry
> Get on your horse
> There's not a moment to lose   } (*Spoken.*)
> This is the golden opportunity
> You simply can't refuse

JANE.
> You're right, Mother.

MRS. BENNET.
> Don't listen to your father
> Don't listen to your sister
> I don't care if their advice is sound
> It's I who protects you
> I who directs you
> I who makes the world go round.
>
> As long as there's a mother
> The sun will shine
> The grass will grow
> As long as there's a mother
> A rose will bloom
> A babbling brook will flow
> And the flags will proudly wave
> The cannons loudly boom
> The world's a finer place because of
> You know whom
> As long as there's a mother
> A child will laugh
> A bird will sing
> And the stars above will twinkle
> And the steeple bells will toll
> The winter wind will whistle
> Through the thistle on the knoll
> The fires of hearth
> Will never smother
> As long as there's a mother.
>
> So hurry, Jane, hurry   (*Spoken to* JANE *as though*
> Get on your horse   *trying to hypnotize her.*

There's not a moment to lose   JANE *stares at her*
This is the golden opportunity   MOTHER.)
You simply can't refuse.

JANE. (*Rises.*) You're right, Mother.

MRS. BENNET.

Though seasons come and seasons go
Do not despair
Your mother dear
Is always there
The tiny chicks cannot survive
Without a hen
A mother hen
Amen.

GIRLS.

As long as there's a mother
The sun will shine
The grass will grow
As long as there's a mother
A rose will bloom
A bubbling brook will flow.

And for every blushing bride
Who finds a handsome groom
A vote of thanks is overdue
As long as there's a mother
To you know whom
A child will laugh
A bird will sing.

Though seasons come and seasons go
Do not despair
Our mother dear
Is always there.

And the hand of nature will provide
For every living thing
The pauper in the poorhouse
God will save the King
There's enough for everybody and his brother.

ALL.

As long as there's a mother.

MUSIC: STOP

(*THUNDER is heard.* MRS. BENNET *kisses* JANE. JANE *and* GIRLS *run off* R. MRS. BENNET *crosses to* D. R.)

MRS. BENNET. (*Singing.*) As long as there's a mother.

MUSIC: 13A

(*She turns, marches off* R.)

(*ENCORE*)

CLOSE IN

ACT ONE

Scene 5

Netherfield Hall. Full stage.

Darcy *and* Bingley *are playing billiards. We hear TWO SNEEZES from Offstage.*

BINGLEY. Poor Miss Jane. Her cold seems to be worse.

(*Sneeze offstage.*)

DARCY. You're just anxious to have her stay on for a while.

BINGLEY. Well, the doctor's advice was that she stay here two or three more days until she has completely recovered.

DARCY. I imagine that you advised the doctor to give that advice.

BINGLEY. She is a charming girl, isn't she?

DARCY. She seems to be unusually attractive for someone of her background. (MISS BINGLEY *enters.*) One game. Then I must finish this letter to my sister.

MISS BINGLEY. Mr. Darcy, please be sure to convey my respects to your dear sister.

DARCY. I shall indeed.

BINGLEY. Oh, Caroline, is Miss Jane feeling better?

MISS BINGLEY. (*Crosses* D. R. *to* C.) Fear not, dear brother. She'll survive. These country people have inhuman constitutions.

BINGLEY. I do hope she isn't planning to leave too soon.

MISS BINGLEY. (*After a look at him.*) I think we can persuade her to stay.

(WILLIAMS, *the butler, enters, stands in doorway.*)

WILLIAMS. Miss Bingley—

MISS BINGLEY. Yes, Williams.

WILLIAMS. There's a lady here, madam.

MISS BINGLEY. A lady?

WILLIAMS. A Miss Elizabeth Bennet.

MISS BINGLEY. (*She looks at the* OTHERS *with amusement.*) Show her in, Williams. A lady? (WILLIAMS *goes.*) Williams is becoming so democratic. (*Crosses* D. L.)

BINGLEY. Caroline, I wouldn't want you to be unkind to her.

MISS BINGLEY. I shall be kindness itself. But I do hope she isn't planning to catch cold, too.

BINGLEY. (*A bit angry.*) Caroline, I don't like— (*Stops talking as* ELIZABETH *enters. She is wearing a cloak and heavy shoes.*

She is carrying some dresses over her arm. They are covered with cloth.)

MISS BINGLEY. Why, Miss Bennet, how nice of you to call.

ELIZABETH. Thank you, Miss Bingley.

BINGLEY. Good afternoon, Miss Bennet.

ELIZABETH. Good afternoon, Mr. Bingley.

DARCY. Miss Bennet.

ELIZABETH. (*After a moment's hesitation.*) Mr. Darcy. I've been anxious to see my sister and I've brought some clothes she asked for in her note. (*She looks down at her shoes, becoming aware that they are a little muddy.*) Please forgive my shoes. I'm afraid they're a bit dusty from the walk.

MISS BINGLEY. You mean you actually walked here? (*Crosses R. to her.*)

ELIZABETH. Our other horse was needed at the farm. I had no alternative but to walk.

MISS BINGLEY. But, how shocking.

DARCY. (*Crosses L.*) Is it shocking for a young lady to be concerned about her sister?

MISS BINGLEY. (*Realizing that she looks bad.*) Come, Miss Elizabeth, let me take you to your sister.

BINGLEY. I hope you can stay for dinner.

ELIZABETH. (*Looking at her clothes.*) I'm afraid I'm not dressed properly for—

BINGLEY. Oh, that doesn't matter.

ELIZABETH. No, really, my clothes—

MISS BINGLEY. Of course, if it would make you uncomfortable, well—

ELIZABETH. (*Looks at* BINGLEY. *She seems to come to a decision out of sheer perversity and amusement.*) I could wear something of Jane's.

BINGLEY. Good.

MISS BINGLEY. Yes, come, let me take you to Jane. (*They start off.*) I'm so happy you can stay.

ELIZABETH. I'm so glad to have made you happy. (*They go.*)

BINGLEY. I've never seen Caroline handled so well. (*Crosses R., sits at table.*) That Miss Elizabeth is a most unusual female.

DARCY. I agree. Most unusual. Fortunately, she doesn't like me.

BINGLEY. Fortunately?

DARCY. Yes, fortunately. Here is a girl with no position—no background, and a dreadful mother. Still, as you say, she is unusual—and has rather fine eyes. And if she liked me, I'd find myself responding.

BINGLEY. (*Sarcastic.*) A horrifying thought.

DARCY. But there's no need to think about it because she dislikes me. She doesn't even seem to care about my money, unlike most women of her class.

BINGLEY. (*Rises, drifts D. L.*) Darcy, how is it possible that I, the most charming of men, can be friends with the biggest snob in Christendom?

DARCY. (*Rising.*) Bingley, pride is not snobbery. A snob is a man who looks up at his betters and down at his equals. He is always uncertain of his position. Not I. I know who I am and what I am, and whenever I have forgotten that, I've had reason to regret it.

BINGLEY. Are you hinting at some secret romp with a chambermaid?

DARCY. Chambermaids are never a problem. Middle-class women are. They require marriage. A marriage should take place only between equals.

BINGLEY. Suppose you were to fall wildly in love?

DARCY. Gentlemen don't fall wildly in love.

BINGLEY. I don't agree. I think I am a gentleman and I think I could fall wildly in love. Regardless of who or what she is.

DARCY. Jane?

MUSIC: 14

BINGLEY. Jane.

(*Song: JANE.*)

BINGLEY.
> Heavenly
> I repeat
> Heavenly
> Soft and sweet
> Every time I hear that voice
> I have to stop . . .
> Music to my ear
>
> Beautiful

DARCY.
> Simply country lass

BINGLEY.
> You'll agree

DARCY.
> So nice and middle class

BINGLEY.
> Beautiful
> When you see
> Paradise on earth
> An angel, an angel
> There's no other word for
>
> Jane
> What a discovery

DARCY.
>   I'll admit she's a very pretty girl

BINGLEY.
>   Jane
>   No chance for recovery

DARCY.
>   You'll get over it.

BINGLEY.
>   I surrender to Jane
>   To Jane because she's
>   Heavenly

DARCY. (*Obbligato.*)
>   And if she proves a bore?

BINGLEY.
>   I repeat
>   Heavenly

DARCY. (*Obbligato.*)
>   You've got the other four

BINGLEY.
>   Soft and sweet
>   Paradise on earth
>   An angel, an angel
>   There's no other way of explaining
>   Beautiful

DARCY. (*Obbligato.*)
>   Don't mention that name again

BINGLEY.
>   What name?

BOTH.
>   Heavenly
>   Jane.

MISS BINGLEY. (*Entering* U. C., *crosses* D. L. *below piano.*) Miss Elizabeth will be down directly.

BINGLEY. Is Miss Jane coming down?

MISS BINGLEY. No, I don't think she's well enough. But you can go sit with her after a while. (ELIZABETH *enters from stairway, crosses Downstage to secretary.*) Ah! (DARCY *and* BINGLEY *rise.*)

DARCY. That suits you.

ELIZABETH. Thank you.

MISS BINGLEY. You look quite presentable now.

BINGLEY. Will you join us in a game of cards?

ELIZABETH. No, thank you. Please don't stop because of me. I'd enjoy looking at some of your books, if I may.

MISS BINGLEY. Miss Elizabeth is a great reader, I'm sure. I imagine an intellectual would find card playing much too frivolous.

ELIZABETH. That's very kind of you, Miss Bingley. But I'm not an intellectual and I do many frivolous things.

MISS BINGLEY. Such as?

ELIZABETH. Such as idle conversation when I might be looking at books.

(DARCY *riffles cards in concealed delight, sits.*)

BINGLEY. (*Going to desk and taking out books.*) Let me help you. I hope you found your sister improved.

ELIZABETH. Oh, much, thank you. I think she may be taken home soon.

BINGLEY. Miss Jane mustn't go out until the doctor advises it. (*Hands her a book.*) There are others in the library if you care for none of these.

ELIZABETH. No, this will suit me perfectly, thank you. (*Sits down and starts reading.* BINGLEY *goes back to card table and picks up cards.*)

BINGLEY. Shall we go on, Darcy?

DARCY. (*Rising.*) No. You play with Miss Bingley. I must finish this letter to my sister. (*He goes* R. *to secretary, sits and takes up quill.*)

MISS BINGLEY. How I long to see your sister again. (*Crosses* L. *to table, sits.*) She is truly a delight. Such a countenance—such manners—and so extremely accomplished for one her age.

BINGLEY. It seems to me these days all young ladies are accomplished to a remarkable degree.

MISS BINGLEY. Charles! All young ladies?

BINGLEY. (*Nodding.*) I don't know where they get the patience.

MISS BINGLEY. Do you agree, Mr. Darcy?

DARCY. Do I agree with what?

MISS BINGLEY. Charles feels that all young ladies are accomplished.

DARCY. I can't say that I know more than half a dozen who really are.

MISS BINGLEY. Nor I. What do you think, Miss Elizabeth?

ELIZABETH. Not being an accomplished young lady, I wouldn't know what makes one.

MISS BINGLEY. (*Rises, crosses* L. *to* ELIZABETH.) No young lady can be remotely thought accomplished unless she has a thorough knowledge of music, singing, dancing, and foreign languages. *N'est-ce pas?*

ELIZABETH. *Oui.*

BINGLEY. Caroline, are we playing or aren't we?

MISS BINGLEY. Oh, I don't wish to play cards, Charles. I think I would prefer a book, too. After all, there's no enjoyment like reading.

ELIZABETH. Here, Miss Bingley, I think you will enjoy this. (*Handing* MISS BINGLEY *the book.*) I'll play with you, Mr. Bingley.

MISS BINGLEY. Thank you. (*After a pause.*) Miss Elizabeth, do you play?

ELIZABETH. Play?

MISS BINGLEY. The pianoforte.

ELIZABETH. A little.

MISS BINGLEY. Really! Charles, perhaps you are right about all young ladies being accomplished. Do you sing, too?

ELIZABETH. A little.

MISS BINGLEY. Isn't that marvelous? Will you do something for us?

ELIZABETH. If you don't mind, I'd rather not.

MISS BINGLEY. Oh, come, Miss Elizabeth. Shyness is the last thing I'd expect from you.

BINGLEY. Caroline—

MISS BINGLEY. Mr. Darcy, I'm sure if you asked Miss Elizabeth to play, she would.

(*There is an uncomfortable pause.* ELIZABETH *stops playing cards and sits, waiting.* DARCY *seems to be making a decision. Finally he speaks in a warm, friendly voice.*)

DARCY. (*Rising.*) Miss Elizabeth, if you would care to play something, I should be most happy to hear it.

EIZABETH. (*She gets up as though obeying a command, seats herself at piano. She plays an arpeggio.*) What would you like to hear?

BINGLEY. Oh, anything. Anything at all.

ELIZABETH. This is one of my father's favorites.

MUSIC: 15

(*She plays and sings "LOVE WILL FIND OUT THE WAY."*)

>The road of love
>The road of love
>Is often a troublesome journey
>As winding, wand'ring as the road
>From Uxbridge to Tunbridge to Selsey by the sea.
>
>But love will find out the way
>Love will find out the way
>Though winding and wand'ring the road may be
>Love will find out the way
>
>To reach the heart
>To reach the heart
>Is often a worrisome journey
>As twisting, turning as the road
>From Uxbridge to Tunbridge to Selsey by the sea.

But love will find out the way
Love will find out the way
Though twisting and turning the road may be
Love will find out the way.

(After song.)

DARCY. I enjoyed it very much.
ELIZABETH. Thank you.
BINGLEY. Delightful. Delightful.
MISS BINGLEY. Excellent.
BINGLEY. You know, music cheers this old place up. (*Rises. Crosses L. to piano.*) I'll tell you what. As soon as your sister has recovered, I shall give a party. What do you think, Caroline?
MISS BINGLEY. (*Starts off R.*) It might be pleasant, providing we are careful about whom we invite.
BINGLEY. (*Crosses U. L. to end of piano.*) Oh, we'll have our neighbors and the officers from the regiment.

(DARCY *turns away.* ELIZABETH *watches him.*)

MISS BINGLEY. Not all the officers, Charles. I must see about dinner. (*She exits R.*)
BINGLEY. I must tell Miss Jane about the party. (*He starts off, stops.*) What did Caroline mean, "Not all the officers"? (*Suddenly looks at* DARCY.) Oh, Wickham. (*He goes upstairs.*)
ELIZABETH. (*Angrily imitating him.*) "Oh, Wickham." Mr. Darcy, I don't understand—
DARCY. (*Interrupting her.*) Miss Elizabeth, I do not wish to be rude, but I don't care to discuss Wickham.
ELIZABETH. Well, may I ask you a hypothetical question?
DARCY. If you like.
ELIZABETH. What would you think of a man who had everything the world has to offer—birth, breeding, wealth, good looks— (*She sizes him up.*) even charm, when he chose to exercise it— What would be your opinion of a man with such gifts who refused to accept an introduction to a man who was poor and of no consequence? And who acts as though that man were non-existent? Not even worth—

(MISS BINGLEY *has entered and is standing Upstage of them.*)

DARCY. (*Interrupting.*) Miss Elizabeth, I should reserve my opinion until I knew the circumstances of the particular case.
ELIZABETH. Do you suppose that if the gentleman were asked, he would reveal those circumstances?
DARCY. No. A gentleman doesn't have to explain his actions.

He expects people to give him credit for being a man of honor and integrity.

MISS BINGLEY. I feel that I should tell Miss Elizabeth—

DARCY. (*Attempting to stop her.*) Please, Miss Bingley—

MISS BINGLEY. No. I feel this is my duty. I know that George Wickham goes about saying that he has been ill used by you. (*To* ELIZABETH.) Well, Miss Elizabeth, while I am ignorant of the particulars, I know that what Wickham says is not true.

ELIZABETH. How clever of you, my dear Miss Bingley, to know something of which you are ignorant.

MISS BINGLEY. I have always found Wickham to be a man of absolutely no principle. But there—what can you expect of a man of his low descent? (*Crosses* D. L.)

ELIZABETH. I'll tell you exactly what I expect. Kindness, honor, generosity, truthfulness! (*She starts off, stops.*) And I might add that I expect precisely the same from persons of high descent. I'm going to see my sister. (*She starts off again.*)

MISS BINGLEY. Such insolence and bad manners.

DARCY. Miss Bingley, I think the bad manners are not Miss Bennet's. (MISS BINGLEY *turns, exits* L.) I admired you for that.

ELIZABETH. You admired me?

DARCY. Yes, even though I was the victim of your attack, I admired you for it. I think your resentment of what you believed to be an injustice showed courage and loyalty. Miss Elizabeth— (*Crosses* L. *toward* ELIZABETH.) I wish I might have a friend who could defend me as ably and earnestly as you defended Wickham.

ELIZABETH. (*Flustered.*) I—I had better go and see my sister. (*She exits up stairway, stops halfway up stairs, looks at* DARCY, *then goes.*)

DARCY. (*He watches her leave, then strolls over to the piano, looks at it.*) From Uxbridge, to Tunbridge, to Selsey-by-the-Sea—

                                                        MUSIC: 16

(*He goes into song "A GENTLEMAN."*)

Yes, I liked the impromptu concert
The singing was rather nice
But that's not sufficient reason
For ignoring my own advice.

Yes, I thought she was most impressive
The manner, the poise, the grace
But such things are best not thought of
Or a man could forget his place.

When one meets a woman
One has to examine her family ties
One should be looking at the facts

And not the eyes
And not the eyes.

A gentleman never falls wildly in love
A gentleman upholds his dignity and name.

He knows who he is
He knows what he is
And if he forgets
He'll only have himself to blame.

A gentleman never gets carried away.

(*Walks* U. L., *circles pool table, starts upstairs, pauses, walks* D. R. *to table, continues dialogue.*)

Lovely
Different

A gentleman never falls wildly in love

Never!

CLOSE IN

ACT ONE

SCENE 6

Exterior Longbourn, in One. MR. BENNET *is working on his hedge.* ELIZABETH *and* MRS. BENNET *enter from* R. 1.

MUSIC: 16A

MR. BENNET. Oh, you're back. (*He embraces Mrs. Bennet.*) Where's Jane?

ELIZABETH. She's gone straight to her room, Papa. But she is feeling much better.

MRS. BENNET. I'm so glad I drove over myself to fetch Jane. If only to see the look in Mr. Bingley's eyes when he assisted her into the carriage. Dear Mr. Bingley, what a charming son-in-law he will be.

MR. BENNET. He hasn't proposed yet, has he?

MRS. BENNET. No, but he will. (*Crosses* D. L.) Oh, it has all turned out so beautifully. Such a clever idea of mine, sending Jane over to Netherfield in the rain.

ELIZABETH. Yes, Mama, but Jane should get some credit for having caught the cold.

MRS. BENNET. Of course. One can't do everything alone.

MR. BENNET. Lizzie, it's too bad you couldn't manage to get a cold of your own and stay long enough to get engaged to Mr. Darcy.

MRS. BENNET. Hmph. That Mr. Darcy, looking down his nose at everyone. (*Crosses* R. *between* ELIZABETH *and* MR. BENNET.) I set him right. Did you hear what I said to him, Lizzie?

ELIZABETH. Yes, I heard only too clearly.

MR. BENNET. What did you say?

MRS. BENNET. Oh, I merely mentioned the fact that there are some gentlemen who are gentlemen without being gentlemen. Whereas, many a gentleman who is not a gentleman may be a gentleman. It shattered him.

MR. BENNET. It has me a bit shaky, myself.

(MR. BENNET *starts off* C. COLLINS *enters* C.)

COLLINS. Mr. Bennet.

MR. BENNET. (*Nodding to* COLLINS.) Mr. Collins. (*He goes.*)

COLLINS. (*Crosses* R. *to* MRS. BENNET.) Madam, may I have your permission to solicit a private interview with your daughter Elizabeth?

MRS. BENNET. A private interview? Indeed, you have my blessing.

ELIZABETH. Mama, Mr. Collins can have nothing private to say to me.

MRS. BENNET. No nonsense, Lizzie. I desire you to stay where you are.

COLLINS. Pray, madam, do not be severe with her. It is merely her charming modesty.

MRS. BENNET. Her charming modesty.

(*She goes.* ELIZABETH *and* COLLINS *are alone. She is avoiding his eyes. He is looking at her with fatuous approval.*)

ELIZABETH. Mr. Collins, I'm sorry, but——

COLLINS. Pray, do not apologize. Your innocent modesty does you no disservice in my eyes. It somehow adds to your other perfections. Miss Elizabeth— (*Crosses* D. L.) almost the very moment that I set foot into this house I singled you out as the companion of my future life.

ELIZABETH. Mr. Collins! (*Crosses* L. *to him.*)

COLLINS. Now, now— (*Raises hand to stop* ELIZABETH.) before we permit our deep feeling to run away with us, let me state my reasons for marrying. First, I—

ELIZABETH. Mr. Collins you are too hasty, sir. You forget that

I have made no answer. I appreciate the honor of your proposal, but I cannot accept.

COLLINS. I rather expected that. I understand that it is a delicate custom for young ladies to say no when they secretly mean yes.

ELIZABETH. I am not such a young lady, Mr. Collins. I mean no.

COLLINS. I cannot believe you would actually reject such an opportunity. You know, Miss Elizabeth, you may never receive another marriage proposal. After all, you are penniless. Look at me. (*Crosses* L. *towards* ELIZABETH.) Tell me that you will marry me.

ELIZABETH. Well, Mr. Collins, let's put it this way—I'd rather die.

COLLINS. You are absolutely charming. (ELIZABETH *starts off* L.) Like all females, you want to be wooed—ardently. Let me pour out to you my words of love.

MUSIC: 17

(*Lead into "NO."*)

    Fragrant flower
    Tiny tulip
    By love consumed
    Here I stand
    I stand, I stand in all humility
    to offer you my hand
    Say the word to fill my heart and yours with joy.

ELIZABETH. (*Rises, as* COLLINS *offers hand. She rejects it.*)
    No, no, no, etc.

COLLINS.
    Lovely lily
    Bashful buttercup
    How disarming of you to first refuse
    The man you secret, secret, secret, secretly
    Long to choose (*Kneels.*)

ELIZABETH.
    No, no, no, etc.
            (*Crosses* L. *of* COLLINS *then* D. L.)

COLLINS.
    Fiery fuchsia
    Gentle jasmine
    How charming the feminine touch
    Of prolonging
    Sweet suspense, suspense, suspense so much
(COLLINS *follows* L., *catches* ELIZABETH, *crosses her* D. R. C.)
    The sweet suspense prepares me for acceptance.

ELIZABETH.

No, no, no, no, no, no, no, etc.

            (ELIZABETH *backs* COLLINS D. L.)

COLLINS.

Hey!

Lilac

          (*Crosses* R. *to* ELIZABETH, *offers* R. *hand*.)

ELIZABETH.

No, no, no, no. (*She rejects* COLLINS.)

COLLINS.

Crocus (L. *hand.*)

ELIZABETH.

No, no, no, no

COLLINS.

Iris (R. *hand.*)

ELIZABETH.

No, no, no, no

COLLINS.

Daisy (L. *hand.*)

ELIZABETH.

No, no, no, no . . . no, no, no.

COLLINS.

Daffodil

ELIZABETH.

No, no, no, no.

COLLINS.

Dandelion

ELIZABETH.

No, no, no, no, no.

COLLINS.

Bachelor's button? (*Stumbles* D. R.)

ELIZABETH.

No! (*She crosses* L., *sits on bench.*)

COLLINS.

I know you want me (*Crosses* L. *to bench.*)

I know, I know, I know . . . (*Sits on bench.*)

ELIZABETH.

No! (ELIZABETH *rises and bends over* COLLINS. *He falls back on bench.*)

No!

    (*She exits* U. L. *hurriedly, followed by* COLLINS.)

                         MUSIC: 17A

ACT ONE

Scene 7

MUSIC: 18

Full stage. Garden at Netherfield Hall. Party is in progress. On rise, People *are posed.* Mrs. Bennet *enters from* l., *crosses* r. *to* Miss Bingley.

(Collins *enters from* l.)

Collins. Miss Elizabeth—Miss Elizabeth—

Mrs. Bennet. (*Crosses* l. *to* Collins.) Ah, Mr. Collins. Are you enjoying the party?

Collins. Very much. It was so kind of Mr. Bingley to invite me. I was looking for Miss Elizabeth. We are to have the next dance, but she seems to be avoiding me.

Mrs. Bennet. Oh, Mr. Collins, you know the way of a maid with a man.

Collins. No, I don't. Perhaps I'll dance with someone else. (*Crosses* r.)

Mrs. Bennet. (*Stops* Collins.) Wait, let me find you a partner. Someone safe. That is, someone nice. (*She sees* Lady Lucas *and* Charlotte *enter* r.) Ah, there's Charlotte. She's very plain but they tell me she dances quite smoothly.

Collins. If you don't mind, Mrs. Bennet, I'd—

Mrs. Bennet. (*Crosses* r. *to* Lady Lucas *and* Charlotte.) Charlotte, Mr. Collins is most anxious to have the next dance with you.

Lady Lucas. Charlotte will be most happy to dance with Mr. Collins.

(Charlotte *and* Collins *exit* u. r. Jane *and* Bingley *come down to* c. *through dancers. She sings.*)

Jane.
　　"Though twisting and turning the road may be,
　　　Love will find out the way . . ."

Mrs. Bennet. (*To* Lady Lucas.) Love will find out the way if you give it a little push. (*They exit through the garden* u. r.)

Jane. Mr. Bingley, don't you think you had better spend some time with your other guests?

Bingley. Are you growing weary of me?

Jane. Oh, no. But it would be unkind of me to keep you to myself.

Bingley. Very— (*Bows, starts off.*)

JANE. (*Stopping him.*) But it would be unkind to myself to let you go.

BINGLEY. Very unkind.

MUSIC: 19

(JANE *and* BINGLEY *do number:* "*I FEEL SORRY FOR THE GIRL WHO HASN'T GOT A BEAU.*")

BINGLEY.
> I consider myself your companion
> Your escort
> Your beau
> I intend to devote all my time to you.

JANE.
> I confess I'm excited
> I'm delighted
> I'm flattered
> And I'm happy too.

> I feel sorry for the girl who hasn't got a beau
> Hasn't got a beau
> What a situation
> 'Specially in the springtime
> Fee fi fo fum.

> I feel sorry for the girl who hasn't got the spark
> Hasn't got the spark
> Or the inclination
> Ever to have a fling
> Fee fi fo
> Fumbling
> What's the use of
> Fumbling
> What's the use of stumbling
> When it's such a wonderful day to make hay.

> I feel sorry for the girl who hasn't got a beau
> Hasn't got a beau
> Oh, what desperation
> What a catastrophe
> Fi fo fum
> What a day to fall in love.

BINGLEY.
> I feel sorry for the girl who hasn't got a beau
> Hasn't got a beau
> What a situation

'Specially in the springtime
Fee fi fo fum.

I feel sorry for the girl who hasn't got the spark
Hasn't got the spark
Or the inclination
Ever to have a fling.

(*Speaks.*) What a day to fall in love!

(*Dance sequences follow*—KITTY *and* ROCKINGHAM, MARY *and*
LT. DENNY, LYDIA *and* WICKHAM. MARY *exits.*)

MUSIC: 19A

(CHORUS *sing their section of "I FEEL SORRY"—dances follow,
with* KITTY *and* LT. ROCKINGHAM, LT. DENNY *and* MARY,
LYDIA *and* CAPTAIN WICKHAM. CHORUS *finishes "I FEEL
SORRY FOR THE GIRL."* DARCY *enters from* L., JANE *and*
BINGLEY *cross to* MISS BINGLEY, *who has come on from* R.)

BINGLEY. I think I'll show Miss Jane the rest of the grounds—
show her the shrubbery. We have some marvelous shrubbery.
(*They exit.*)

MISS BINGLEY. (*To* DARCY.) I'm afraid that tender little
romance is getting a bit sticky. Frankly, Mr. Darcy, I couldn't
bear this place were it not for you.

DARCY. You are too kind.

MISS BINGLEY. I'm quite sincere. The only redeeming feature
of this whole ghastly expedition has been the fact that I have been
able to become closer friends with you. Heavens, I'm talking like
one of these brazen country girls. What will you think of me?

DARCY. (*Set smile.*) My opinion of you, Miss Bingley, will
never change.

(WICKHAM *enters* D. R. *1, crosses* C., *hesitates as he sees them.*
DARCY *turns away.*)

WICKHAM. (*To* MISS BINGLEY.) I am looking for Miss Eliza-
abeth.

MISS BINGLEY. I'm sure you will find her. (WICKHAM *bows and
goes* U. C. *To* DARCY.) I'm sorry we had to ask Wickham here.
He's second in command of the Regiment and it would have been
an affront to ask the other officers and not him. High treason, or
something. But we shan't see much of him. He will be occupying
himself with Miss Elizabeth.

DARCY. Oh?

MISS BINGLEY. Oh, yes. The last time they were together I

noticed that she was quite taken with him. (DARCY *looks at her sharply*.) A woman can always tell these things. (ELIZABETH *and* WICKHAM *enter from* L. *They stroll Upstage; cross Downstage to* L., *sit on bench. Indicating* ELIZABETH *and* WICKHAM *with her hand*.) There, you see, Mr. Darcy? (DARCY *looks and says nothing*.) She is taken with him. I just can't conceive of a woman who could find George Wickham attractive and dislike someone like you so intensely.

DARCY. She—uh—does dislike me, doesn't she?

MISS BINGLEY. It's quite apparent, isn't it? Charles told me you yourself noticed it. He noticed it. And of course I noticed it.

DARCY. How nice that we all agree. (*Exits* R. 1.)

(MISS BINGLEY *exits* U. R.)

WICKHAM. (*To* ELIZABETH.) I suppose they consider it beastly of me to have come, but I wouldn't give Darcy the satisfaction of staying away.

ELIZABETH. Captain Wickham, I have spoken to Mr. Darcy and he didn't seem the sort of man who would have done anything that would—

WICKHAM. (*Cutting in*.) I can see that Mr. Darcy has fooled you as he has fooled everyone else. (*Paces few steps* R., *turns back*.) Miss Elizabeth, would it surprise you to learn that I was once intended for the church?

ELIZABETH. Really? You seem so well-fitted for the army.

WICKHAM. I have no taste for soldiering. The church should have been my profession and it would have been, if Darcy had not arranged to stop me.

ELIZABETH. He stopped you?

WICKHAM. When Mr. Darcy's father died, he left an annuity to me, provided I entered the church. But Darcy refused to give me the money.

ELIZABETH. I knew Mr. Darcy was proud and arrogant. I can't imagine him dishonorable.

WICKHAM. He should be publicly exposed. But as long as I remember the father, I can never bring myself to disgrace the son.

(LYDIA *enters from* U. L. *as MUSIC starts*.)

MUSIC: 20

ELIZABETH. I admire your generosity, Captain Wickham.

LYDIA. (*Interrupting*.) Come on, Wickie, this is our dance. I won't let Lizzie monopolize you.

WICKHAM. You will forgive me, Miss Elizabeth, but this brat is very insistent.

ELIZABETH. I understand.

(*They join the MAYPOLE DANCE.* COLLINS *enters from* R., *looking for* ELIZABETH.)

COLLINS. Miss Elizabeth—Miss Elizabeth— Excuse me, has anyone seen Miss Elizabeth? (ELIZABETH *exits* U. L.)

OPEN CHANGE

ACT ONE

✦   SCENE 8

Exterior of Netherfield. Target set Stage R.

ELIZABETH *hurries across Stage,* L. *to* R. COLLINS *follows a moment later.*

COLLINS. (*Calling.*) There you are, my flower! (*Exits* R. DARCY *enters* L., *takes up bow and arrow, prepares to shoot.* COLLINS' *voice may be heard Offstage.*) Miss Elizabeth— (ELIZABETH *enters hurriedly from* R., *stops in front of* DARCY. *She ducks into hedge opening* C., *hiding from* COLLINS, *who enters from* R. *Calling.*) Miss Elizabeth— (*To* DARCY.) I beg your pardon, sir. Have you seen Miss Elizabeth Bennet?

MUSIC STOPS: 20

DARCY. (*After a moment's hesitation.*) No, I haven't. Perhaps you had better try the other side of the grounds.
COLLINS. Thank you. (*Starts off* L., *stops.*) I beg your pardon, but you look very familiar. Aren't you— (*Hesitates.*)
DARCY. (*Indicating the bow and arrow.*) I'll give you a hint. I steal from the rich and I give to the poor.
COLLINS. Ah, yes. (*Starts off, stops, looks at* DARCY, *puzzled, then goes off,* L., *calling.*) Miss Elizabeth.
ELIZABETH. (*Coming out of hiding. She suddenly covers her mouth to hide a giggle.*) "I steal from the rich and give to the poor." You know, Mr. Darcy, I never would have suspected you of having a sense of humor.
DARCY. (*Looking at her steadily.*) I imagine you wouldn't suspect me of anything worthwhile.
ELIZABETH. (*After returning his look for a moment.*) Well, thank you for helping me, Mr. Darcy. (*She starts off, crosses* D. R.)
DARCY. Miss Elizabeth— (*She stops and looks at him. He crosses* D. R. *to her.*) Miss Elizabeth, I've come to a decision. I decided that I don't want you to dislike me.
ELIZABETH. Oh?
DARCY. (*Suddenly angry.*) It's damned annoying.
ELIZABETH. Damned annoying?

DARCY. (*Suddenly apologetic.*) Oh, forgive me.

ELIZABETH. I don't mind the word "damned." But "annoying." Why should you care whether I like you or not?

DARCY. I don't know why, but I do.

ELIZABETH. Mr. Darcy, are you suddenly in the mood to give consequence to the middle class at play? (DARCY *looks at her.*) I overheard you that evening.

DARCY. (*Crosses L. C. towards her.*) That's why you wouldn't dance with me. (ELIZABETH *nods.*) I wish you would forget that.

ELIZABETH. Is that an order?

DARCY. I don't think you are a woman who responds to orders. I think you act with your mind and your heart. And I believe it is a good mind and a good heart.

ELIZABETH. Mr. Darcy, this is all very puzzling—almost unnerving.

DARCY. (*Smilingly confident.*) Would you care for a little target practice to calm you down?

ELIZABETH. I'm not sure.

DARCY. Archery is a fine old sport and one in which even a young lady can become proficient. (*Crosses L. around her.*)

ELIZABETH. So I've heard.

DARCY. Providing there is a short range and a light bow. Now the left arm must be straight, straight, very straight. (*He shows her how to hold the bow and in so doing he puts his arm around her pretty tightly.*) You know, Miss Elizabeth, at this moment it is very difficult to believe that you are so prejudiced.

ELIZABETH. (*Looking at him.*) At this moment it is very difficult to believe that you are so proud.

MUSIC: 21

(*Lead into duet, "I SUDDENLY FIND IT AGREEABLE."*)

ELIZABETH. (*Spoken.*) After you.

DARCY. (*Spoken.*) No, after you.

ELIZABETH.
>You seem just a trifle too dignified
>Aloof and reserved to the core
>In fact it's a bit of a bore
>But I suddenly find it agreeable

DARCY.
>Agreeable

ELIZABETH.
>Agreeable
>I find it extremely agreeable

DARCY.
>Your manners are rather uncivilized
>You make such an awful to-do
>In short you're a bit of a shrew
>But I suddenly find it agreeable

ELIZABETH.
> Agreeable

DARCY.
> Agreeable
> I find it extremely agreeable

BOTH.
> How fine, how nice, how perfectly grand
> To think we can make amends
> Especially since
> We both have displayed
> Talent for not making friends

DARCY.
> At first blush I thought you impossible
> Your charm failed to come shining through

ELIZABETH.
> I felt quite the same about you

BOTH.
> But I suddenly find it agreeable
> Agreeable
> Agreeable

ELIZABETH.
> How fine—

DARCY.
> How nice—

ELIZABETH. That we—agree.

ELIZABETH. (*Spoken.*)
> On second thought

DARCY. (*Spoken.*)
> I had some second thoughts myself, Miss Elizabeth

ELIZABETH. (*Spoken.*)
> After you.

DARCY. (*Spoken.*)
> No, after you.

ELIZABETH. (*Sung.*)
> I once thought your wealth was a detriment
> You seemed such a snob all along
> I'm still not convinced I was wrong

DARCY.
> But you suddenly find it agreeable

ELIZABETH.
> Agreeable

DARCY.
> Agreeable

ELIZABETH.
> I find it extremely agreeable

DARCY.
> I've met any number of families

From London to Brittany shores
And I've never seen one like yours

ELIZABETH.
But you suddenly find it agreeable

DARCY.
Agreeable

ELIZABETH.
Agreeable
How fine,

DARCY.
How nice, how perfectly grand
We've finally called a halt
Especially since you have to agree

BOTH. (*Spoken.*)
The whole thing was mostly your fault

ELIZABETH.
This meeting was quite unforeseeable
I'd not seek you out on my own

DARCY. (*Spoken.*)
I'd much rather be here alone

But I suddenly find it agreeable
Agreeable—agreeable

ELIZABETH.
How fine—

DARCY.
How nice—

ELIZABETH.
How sweet—

DARCY.
How grand— That we agree

ELIZABETH.
That we agree. . . .

(*After song:*)

Mr. Darcy, how did you say I should hold my arm? (*Crosses* R. *towards quiver.*)

DARCY. Straight, straight, very straight. Miss Elizabeth, why don't we slip away from this party and go for a drive?

ELIZABETH. (*Liking it, but slightly hesitant.*) Well—

DARCY. I don't know the countryside 'round here. I'm suddenly interested in seeing it.

ELIZABETH. I'd like to show it to you.

DARCY. I'll arrange for a carriage. (*Starting off* L.) Madam, do not stir from this spot.

ELIZABETH. (*Obediently.*) No, sir, I won't.

MUSIC: 22

(*He goes* L. ELIZABETH *sings "THIS REALLY ISN'T ME."*)

ELIZABETH.
>This really isn't me
>Not the girl I know so well
>And yet I must confess I like the change
>
>This simply cannot be
>Things should never go so well
>The clouds beneath my feet seem rather strange
>
>My head is much too light
>My heart is much too gay
>I'm very unaccustomed to this way
>
>No, this really isn't me
>But I like it oh so well
>So well that I don't care what may befall
>
>I discovered him
>And suddenly you see
>This really isn't me at all
>
>How fine how nice
>How perfectly grand
>To think we could make amends
>Especially since
>It's perfectly clear
>We always were meant to be friends
>
>This really isn't me
>But I like it oh so well
>So well that I don't care what may befall
>
>I discovered him
>And suddenly you see
>This really isn't me at all.
>It isn't me at all.

(*After song:* JANE *and* BINGLEY *enter.*)

JANE. Lizzie, Mr. Bingley is going to arrange a Highland Reel for us.

BINGLEY. Do come along. We'll find you a partner, Miss Elizabeth.

(DARCY *enters during above speech from* L.)

ELIZABETH. Well—
DARCY. Miss Elizabeth has a partner. We're going for a drive.
JANE. Oh!
BINGLEY. Oh!

(JANE *goes off, followed by* BINGLEY. BINGLEY *stops for a moment, looks at* ELIZABETH *and* DARCY.)

DARCY. (*To* ELIZABETH.) You would prefer the drive?
ELIZABETH. Yes, I would.
DARCY. Shall we?

(BINGLEY *goes.* DARCY *gives* ELIZABETH *his arm. They start* L. MRS. BENNET *and* LADY LUCAS *appear in the archway. They don't see* ELIZABETH *and* DARCY.)

MRS. BENNET. Lady Lucas, did you see them, Jane and Mr. Bingley? The way they were looking at each other?
LADY LUCAS. Well, he makes no secret of his admiration.
MRS. BENNET. He adores her, as I knew he would. All that she needed to complete the conquest was that wonderful cold she caught. Wasn't it clever of me to send her over to Netherfield in the rain? (DARCY *and* ELIZABETH *are listening.*) And of course I know once Jane is married to Mr. Bingley, she will see to it that the other girls have the opportunity of meeting all sorts of rich young men. (LADY LUCAS *sees* DARCY. MRS. BENNET *sees* LADY LUCAS *looking at him, turns.*) Just out for a breath of air. (MRS. BENNET *and* LADY LUCAS *exit.*)
ELIZABETH. (*With a sigh.*) Shall we go for that drive? (DARCY *is silent.*) Or would you rather not?
DARCY. As a matter of fact, I don't think it's a good idea for me to leave the party.
ELIZABETH. How fine. How nice.
DARCY. I'm sorry.

MUSIC: 23

(*ORCHESTRA plays the reel music.*)

ELIZABETH. (*Sadly.*) There's the reel. It's such gay music.
DARCY. Yes, isn't it? Let me take you inside.
ELIZABETH. And find me a partner?
DARCY. I'm sure there are many young men eager to dance with you.
ELIZABETH. No, thank you, Mr. Darcy. I prefer to go on with my archery lesson. By myself. (*She fits arrow into bow.* DARCY *bows and exits* L. *1.*) Mr. Fitzwilliam Darcy. (*She shoots.*)

MUSIC: 24

DIM

CLOSE IN

ACT ONE

Scene 9

Interior, Longbourn. Mr. Bennet *is discovered on rise. Offstage from the garden we hear* Mr. Collins *singing.*

Mr. Collins' Voice.
    Fragrant flower
    Tiny tulip
Elizabeth.
    No!

        (Collins *is seen through window* R. C.)

Collins.
    Miss Elizabeth. . . . Miss Elizabeth! (*Crosses* R. 5.)

        (Mrs. Bennet *enters hurriedly from garden* U. C.)

Mrs. Bennet. (*Crosses* D. R. *to* Mr. Bennet.) Mr. Bennet! Mr. Bennet! This is intolerable! Lizzie has refused to marry Mr. Collins again.

Mr. Bennet. I know, Mrs. Bennet.

Mrs. Bennet. You know? Then why aren't you doing something?

Mr. Bennet. Do you want me to thrash her?

Mrs. Bennet. I want you to force her to change her mind immediately or Mr. Collins will change his and not have her at all.

Mr. Bennet. Mrs. Bennet, I would rather not disturb Elizabeth now. She seems troubled enough. I think this Collins matter can wait.

Mrs. Bennet. It cannot wait. You must speak to her. Now. Tell her you insist upon her marrying him.

Mr. Bennet. (*Crosses* R. *to door, calling.*) Lizzie. Lizzie—

Elizabeth. (*She enters* R.) Yes, Papa.

Mr. Bennet. Elizabeth, your mother insists that you marry Mr. Collins.

Mrs. Bennet. (*Turns away.*) Or I shall never see her again.

Mr. Bennet. (*Crosses* L. *a step.*) Elizabeth, an unhappy alternative is before you. Your mother will never see you again if you do not marry Mr. Collins. And I will never see you again if you do.

Elizabeth. Dear Father. (*They embrace.*)

Mrs. Bennet. (*Crosses* R. *to* Mr. Bennet. *Stunned.*) Oh, this is insupportable. How can you do this to your own daughter?

Mr. Bennet. Because I love her. (*He goes off.*)

MRS. BENNET. Oh, that man. Oh, that man.

ELIZABETH. I think he's wonderful, Mama.

MRS. BENNET. Elizabeth Bennet— (*Crosses* R. *to* ELIZABETH.) let me tell you something. (*Crosses* L.) Some day when you are an old maid and I am an old grandmother with no grandchildren— you'll see.

(LYDIA *hurries in, followed by* KITTY *and* MARY. LYDIA *is carrying a sealed envelope.*)

LYDIA. Mama, it's a letter from Netherfield for Jane.

KITTY. It was brought by Mr. Bingley's footman.

MARY. In livery.

MRS. BENNET. (*Taking letter and holding it to her heart.*) It's his proposal. I know it, I know it. Where's Jane?

LYDIA. She's in Maryton. She will be back in a little while.

MRS. BENNET. (*Hugging the letter.*) His proposal. Oh, girls, Jane is going to be Mrs. Charles Bingley. And what that is going to mean for all of us. One can't do everything alone. (*She starts opening the letter.*) I must see what's in this letter.

ELIZABETH. Mama, you have no right to open Jane's letter.

MRS. BENNET. No right to open my own daughter's letter? I never heard of such a thing. Jane wouldn't mind and don't you dare tell her. (*She reads the letter.*) Oh, my God. She has lost him. (*To* ELIZABETH.) You have both lost your husbands.

ELIZABETH. What?

MRS. BENNET. You have thrown away Mr. Collins and now Jane has lost Mr. Bingley. (JANE *enters during this last speech. To* JANE.) Yes, you've lost him. (*Hands* JANE *the letter.*) It's all in this letter which I opened by mistake.

JANE. (*Looking at letter. Crosses* R. *to* ELIZABETH.) This is from Mr. Darcy.

ELIZABETH. (*Taking letter from* JANE.) Mr. Darcy?

MRS. BENNET. (*Rises, crosses to* JANE.) Evil snake.

ELIZABETH. (*Reading from letter.*) "My dear Miss Jane, Mr. Bingley and I have had to leave Netherfield unexpectedly and are not planning to return. He has asked me to write and tell you he will not be able to keep his appointment with you tomorrow."

JANE. We were to go walking.

ELIZABETH. "Please accept my best wishes for yourself and your family." (*Shaking her head.*) Wasn't it enough for him to hurt— (*Putting her arm around* JANE.) Oh, Jane, I'm so sorry.

MRS. BENNET. (*Crosses* D. L.) And there is no proposal at all from Mr. Bingley. After all his compromising attentions to Jane.

ELIZABETH. Mama, he did not compromise Jane.

MRS. BENNET. He's a cruel, undeserving young man. (*She starts off with the* THREE GIRLS. COLLINS *enters from* L.) Mr.

Collins, excuse me. I have one of my headaches. In fact, I have five of them. (*She goes with all* THREE GIRLS.)

COLLINS. What's wrong?

ELIZABETH. It's a private matter, Mr. Collins.

COLLINS. Well, I too have a private matter to discuss. Miss Elizabeth, I have finally decided to accept the fact that you do not wish to marry me.

ELIZABETH. I'm glad of that, Mr. Collins, and I trust you take no offense.

COLLINS. I am not one to take offense at a young woman's foolishness. However, I intend to take my search for a wife else-where. I think in all fairness I should tell you of my plan, because the young lady is a friend of yours. (ELIZABETH *looks at him, puzzled.*) Miss Charlotte Lucas.

JANE. Charlotte!

COLLINS. I intend to call on her today. (COLLINS *dances few steps with himself.*) When I danced with the young lady some days ago I sensed that she did not find me unpleasing. Her family is a good one. Her father is a baronet, which makes it a much more advantageous marriage for me. And furthermore, I feel, if I may say so—

(MRS. BENNET *enters, pulling* MARY *along with her by the hand.*)

MRS. BENNET. Mr. Collins! Mr. Collins, I've decided that Elizabeth is too headstrong and foolish to make you a proper wife. But I do have other kittens in my basket. Don't be shy, Mary.

ELIZABETH. Mama—

MRS. BENNET. Quiet, Lizzie.

ELIZABETH. Mother, I think I should tell you—

MRS. BENNET. (*Going right on.*) Mr. Collins, do you like music? Mary is very musical. (*Pushes* MARY *towards* COLLINS.) Mary, why don't you do something for us?

MARY. (*Balking.*) Mama, please.

MRS. BENNET. (*Shoving her towards harp.*) Go on, dear. (MARY *sits at harp.*) Mary has such beautiful eyes.

COLLINS. Mrs. Bennet, I feel I should tell you—

(MARY *starts singing* "THERE'S A BLUEBIRD IN THE MEADOW.")

MRS. BENNET. Isn't that lovely?

ELIZABETH. (*Very embarrassed.*) Mother, I would like to tell you something.

MRS. BENNET. Quiet, Lizzie.

ELIZABETH. But, Mother, Mr. Collins is on his way to propose to Charlotte.

MRS. BENNET. What's that?

ELIZABETH. I said—

MRS. BENNET. Mary, stop that awful noise! (MARY *stops.*) What's that you're saying, Lizzie?

ELIZABETH. Mr. Collins is on his way to Lucas Lodge to propose marriage to Charlotte.

MRS. BENNET. This is treachery! You, sir, came here expressly to propose to one of my daughters.

COLLINS. I did propose to one of them.

MRS. BENNET. That was Lizzie. Mary won't reject you.

COLLINS. That's what I'm afraid of. (*He bows and goes.*)

MRS. BENNET. Oh, treachery! Oh, villainy! Oh, day of despair!

(KITTY *and* LYDIA *come on in a hurry.*)

LYDIA. What is it, Mama?

MRS. BENNET. Mr. Collins is going to marry Charlotte Lucas.

KITTY. No!

MRS. BENNET. Yes. Elizabeth's best friend has betrayed her.

ELIZABETH. Charlotte doesn't even know about this.

MRS. BENNET. (*Crosses* L. *to sofa, sits.*) Of course she does. She's desperate. Oh, the treachery of the Lucas'. And it's all your fault, Lizzie.

ELIZABETH. Mother, perhaps it isn't my fault— Perhaps— (*Gathering courage.*) Perhaps it's your fault.

MRS. BENNET. (*Majestically.*) My fault—my fault. (*She looks at the other* GIRLS. *They bow their heads as if in agreement with* ELIZABETH.) Oh, I wash my hands of all of you. (*They* ALL *gather around* MOTHER *at sofa.*) You will soon be penniless and I won't care.

ELIZABETH. Ah, Mother dear, you do care and I'm sure you will look after us.

MUSIC: 25

(MRS. BENNET *looks away, angry.* ELIZABETH *starts singing reprise of* "AS LONG AS THERE'S A MOTHER" *and* MRS. BENNET *joins her.*)

MRS. BENNET.	GIRLS.
Though seasons come and seasons go	As long as there's a mother
Do not despair	The sun will shine
Your mother dear	The grass will shine
Is always there	

CURTAIN FALLS

MUSIC: ENTR'ACT: 26

ACT TWO

SCENE 1

MUSIC: 27

Exterior of church in Kent. In One. On Rise we see WEDDING GUESTS *coming out of the church doorway. They will be making various comments, such as "What a charming wedding," "Wasn't the bride lovely," etc.* MRS. BENNET *comes out, followed by* ELIZABETH.

MRS. BENNET. It's amazing what a wedding gown will do for a girl. Even an extremely plain one like Charlotte Lucas.

ELIZABETH. (*She gives her* MOTHER *a nudge because several* GUESTS *are standing close to her.*) Mama!

MRS. BENNET. (*To the Guests.*) I was just saying how lucky Charlotte is. Now that she is Mrs. Collins, she no longer has to worry about her looks.

ELIZABETH. Mama, please!

(ELIZABETH *and* MRS. BENNET *sing* "WASN'T IT A LOVELY WEDDING." *The* OTHERS *join in at various times. At a designated spot in the song,* CHARLOTTE *and* COLLINS *come out of the Church, followed by* LADY LUCAS *and* LORD LUCAS, *and the* GUESTS *turn to look at* CHARLOTTE. *She sings a segment of* "LOVELY WEDDING." *As she finishes her little section,* MRS. BENNET, *overcome by emotion, goes to her, kisses her, then turns and embraces her old acquaintance,* LADY LUCAS. *They* BOTH *wipe the tears from their eyes and exit together. All the other* GUESTS *sing the end of the song.*)

ELIZABETH.
> Wasn't it a simply lovely wedding
> Wasn't he a charming, handsome groom
> Didn't you admire his regal bearing
> As he walked down the aisle.

MRS. BENNET.
> With an odd sort of smile
> Looking like the face of doom

ELIZABETH.
> Wasn't it a truly gay occasion
> Everything a wedding day demands
> How she must have felt to lose her daughter

62

MRS. BENNET.

> How she wept
> Oh, what grief
> Shedding tears
> Of relief
> Glad to get her off her hands

ELIZABETH.

> Oh, there's no sweeter moment in life.

MRS. BENNET.

> Than when beauty and beast become man and wife.

ELIZABETH.

> Wasn't it a simply perfect marriage

MRS. BENNET.

> Wasn't it the kind you dream about

ELIZABETH.

> All together now, let's cheer the couple

MRS. BENNET.

> What's the rush
> Oh my dear
> They won't last
> Through the year

ELIZABETH.

> Everybody shout
> Good luck!

MRS. BENNET.

> Oh, what a bride and groom

ELIZABETH.

> Oh, what a life they'll share

MRS. BENNET.

> Oh, what an ugly pair

ELIZABETH.

> Everybody shout good luck

ALL.

> Good luck.

(CHARLOTTE *and* COLLINS *come out of church, followed by* LADY LUCAS *and* SIR WILLIAM. CHARLOTTE *sings her segment of* WASN'T IT A LIVELY WEDDING.)

MRS. BENNET. (*Embracing* CHARLOTTE.) Charlotte, you were a lovely bride.

(*She goes to* LADY LUCAS, *kisses her and they exit* R. *in tears, followed by* SIR WILLIAM.)

ELIZABETH. (*To* COLLINS *and* CHARLOTTE.) I'd better be going. I know you want to sneak off.

COLLINS. Sneak off?

ELIZABETH. On your honeymoon.

COLLINS. We will do no such thing. First we are invited to lunch at Lady Catherine's.

CHARLOTTE. But, Mr. Collins—dear—

COLLINS. I know, my dear Charlotte, how your little romantic, impatient heart is beating. But we are invited to Lady Catherine de Bourgh's and what can be more important than that?

CHARLOTTE. (*Sighing*.) Nothing.

COLLINS. That's right.

ELIZABETH. Charlotte, you were a beautiful bride.

CHARLOTTE. Thank you, Lizzie dear.

(ELIZABETH *exits* R. CHARLOTTE *and* COLLINS *drift Downstage, exit* R. GUESTS *drift off, singing*.)

CLOSE IN

MUSIC: 28

WEDDING TALK

(CHARLOTTE *and* ENSEMBLE.)

CHARLOTTE.
    Wasn't it a simply lovely wedding?
CHORUS.
    Wasn't she a most enchanting bride?
CHARLOTTE.
    Did you see the preacher almost beaming?
CHORUS.
    When he said "And do you?"
CHARLOTTE.
    And I said "Yes, I do."
    Honestly I could have cried.

CHARLOTTE.

Oh,

There's no sweeter moment in life

Than

When Mister and Miss become Man and Wife

Isn't this a day to dream about

Dear relations?

MEN.

What a lovely Wedding

What a perfect Marriage

Isn't this a simply perfect marriage

Happy friends and neighbors?

GIRLS *and* MEN.
Raise your hats in the air

Give a cheer to the pair
Everybody shout. Good luck.

Oh, there's no sweeter
    moment in life
Than when
    MEN.
Wasn't it a simply
Love . . . ly . . . Wed . . . ding
What a simply perfect mar-
    riage

CHARLOTTE and COLLINS.
Mister and Miss become man
    and wife
GIRLS.
Wasn't it a simply
Lovely wedding?
Wasn't it a day to dream about
Isn't it a simply perfect mar-
    riage.
CHARLOTTE.
Oh, what a handsome groom

GIRLS.
Oh, what a handsome groom

Honestly could have cried
Everybody shout

COLLINS and MEN.
What an enchanting bride
Everybody shout
Good luck.

ACT TWO

SCENE 2

MUSIC: 29

The great hall of Lady Catherine de Bourgh's home in Kent. BUTLER enters, followed by ELIZABETH, MRS. BENNET and COLLINS. MRS. BENNET and ELIZABETH look about the room as ladies do when they first see a place.

BUTLER. Lady Catherine will join you presently.
COLLINS. Please tell her ladyship not to hurry. Miss Lucas— That is, Mrs. Collins—my wife, is freshening up and will be a few minutes.

(BUTLER *bows and goes.*)

MRS. BENNET. What a cozy room.
ELIZABETH. Parliament might feel cozy here.
COLLINS. (*Looking behind him in fright. Crosses* R. C. *to* ELIZABETH.) Miss Elizabeth, please. I wouldn't like Lady Catherine to—
ELIZABETH. I'm sorry, Mr. Collins. A little joke.
COLLINS. One does not joke here. Lady Catherine takes great pride in the fact that she has no sense of humor whatever. This room is large. But it is done in exquisite taste. I am responsible

for much of the decor. (*Looks behind him again.*) Of course, under the guidance of Lady Catherine, whose taste is impeccable. Incidentally, her library is magnificent.

ELIZABETH. I should love to see it.

MRS. BENNET. (*Pointing to a painting.*) Mr. Collins, who is that?

COLLINS. That is my dear patroness' late lamented husband, Lord Alistair de Bourgh. A great nobleman.

MRS. BENNET. How long has he been—?

COLLINS. A few years. He died wearing His Majesty's uniform. Lord de Bourgh was in London watching the triumphant return of Nelson's fleet and he fell out the window of his club.

MRS. BENNET. A hero's death.

ELIZABETH. (*She is looking at another portrait.*) Mr. Collins, isn't that—?

COLLINS. (*Looking at portrait.*) Yes, that is Mr. Darcy as a boy. He's Lady Catherine's favorite nephew. I understand he is going to be here today.

ELIZABETH. Darcy? Here?

COLLINS. It will be quite an honor for Charlotte and myself. And, may I add, for you.

ELIZABETH. Quite an honor, indeed. May I look at the library?

COLLINS. Please do. It's off there. And please be careful of the books. They are a rare treasure. (*He points.*)

ELIZABETH. I shall read them very gently. (*She goes off.*)

MRS. BENNET. (*Looking at another portrait.*) Mr. Collins, who is that?

COLLINS. (*Crosses* R. *to* MRS. BENNET.) That is a portrait of Lady Catherine, herself. Handsome woman, isn't she?

MRS. BENNET. Well, she has a— It's rather a— Well, Mr. Collins.

COLLINS. Beauty isn't everything.

MRS. BENNET. In her case it isn't anything.

COLLINS. (*Paces few steps.*) Mrs. Bennet, you are talking about a great woman whom you are about to meet, and— (*Suddenly switching thoughts, turns.*) Oh, dear. Charlotte is going to be late. I had better go and ask her to hurry. (*Starts off Upstage.*)

MRS. BENNET. (*Crosses* D. L.) The dear girl is probably trying to make herself attractive, and in some cases, that takes time.

COLLINS. I do hope she doesn't try to make herself too attractive. Lady Catherine wouldn't like that. (*Points to portrait.*) She likes to have the distinctions of rank preserved. (*He goes Upstage.*)

MRS. BENNET. Lady Catherine, that man is an ass. (*She turns and looks at Lady Catherine's portrait.*) You don't look very happy. Perhaps it's because you are buried in this mausoleum out here in the country. (*She looks around a moment, then back to portrait.*) Now, when I'm rich—and I will be rich—things will be very different. (*She sings "A HOUSE IN TOWN."*)

MUSIC: 30

My poor, poor family . . . my little dears
How we've suffered and struggled through these lean lean
    years
But I know
The hand of Providence will one day turn the tide
And I will be granted
That wonderful dream
I've always kept inside

A house in town
A house in town
Just a tiny MMM spectacular
house in town
Nothing very much
Just a smashing house in town

A house in town
A house in town
Just a tiny MMM spectacular
House in town
Nothing very much
Just a smashing house in town

I can see it now. . . .
Elegant
Distinguished
Noble
Grand
Poetical
Aesthetical
It covers so much land
Near Bond Street
Or Knightsbridge
Or Grosvenor Square
A view of the palace
From our sitting room chair

A different cook for every meal
To get a change of taste
And footmen standing end to end
Just bowing from the waist

At every turn a marble urn

With ferns of leafy green
Imported from the Orient
Presented by the Queen

A house in town
For dear mama
Just a tiny MMM spectacular
Oo La La
Nothing very much
Just a smashing house in town

Nobility will come from far and near
They'll fight to be invited to the ball of the year

There'll be dancing
There'll be drinking
There'll be caviar
By the ton

Ach du lieber
What a triumph
And the evening's
Just begun

Excitement is growing
The tension is mounting
The glorious moment is here

(Spoken.)
A hush falls over the crowd
A delicate fanfare, not too long, not too soft
All eyes will turn to see
There, poised at the top of the stairs . . . me

Gad, she's beautiful!

A house in town
A house in town
Just a tiny MMM unprecedented
House in town
Nothing very much
Just a dazzling house
A dashing house
A breathless house
A smashing house in town

All mine

All mine
All mine

A house in town!

(*After song, she goes over and looks at Darcy's portrait.*)

I still may get my house in town. (*She crosses and calls* ELIZA-
BETH.) Lizzie, Lizzie, come here.

ELIZABETH. (*Entering.*) That's an excellent library.

MRS. BENNET. Books will get you nowhere. (*Takes book away
from* ELIZABETH, *puts it on piano. Crosses* D. R.) Lizzie, I've been
thinking, as long as Mr. Darcy is going to be here today—perhaps
if you were a little more friendly to him—

ELIZABETH. (*Cutting in.*) Mother, you have always detested
Mr. Darcy. (*Crosses to above piano.*)

MRS. BENNET. Lizzie, he is still single. Therefore, I must submerge my own feelings.

ELIZABETH. Well, I can't submerge mine.

MUSIC: 31

(ELIZABETH *strolls to the piano, sits and starts to play. She plays
"LOVE WILL FIND OUT THE WAY." After a few bars,*
BUTLER *admits* LADY CATHERINE *and her daughter,* ANNE.
LADY CATHERINE *is talking as she enters.* ELIZABETH *stops
playing and rises when she sees* LADY CATHERINE.)

LADY CATHERINE. Well, Collins— (*Looks about her.*) Collins—
Where's Collins?

ELIZABETH. (*Rises, crosses* R.) He went to his cottage to fetch
Charlotte.

LADY CATHERINE. (*Interrupting her.*) Who are you?

ELIZABETH. I am Mr. Collins' cousin, Elizabeth Bennet. And
this is my mother, Mrs. Bennet.

MRS. BENNET. (*Bowing.*) Your Ladyship, this is a great honor.

LADY CATHERINE. I've heard of you Bennets. You are the impoverished ones.

ELIZABETH. Not impoverished, your ladyship.

LADY CATHERINE. Then what are you?

MRS. BENNET. We prefer to think of ourselves as unwealthy.

LADY CATHERINE. As you wish. But I think if persons haven't
the good sense to have money, they should admit it. This is my
daughter, Lady Anne. (ELIZABETH *and* MRS. BENNET *bow.* ANNE
returns the bow.) Anne is shy. (*To* ELIZABETH.) You were playing
when I came in. Please continue.

ELIZABETH. If you don't mind, I'd rather not.

LADY CATHERINE. Nonsense, play. At once.

MRS. BENNET. I am afraid my daughter is a bit shy, too.

LADY CATHERINE. Ridiculous. For a girl of her class, shyness is pure pretension.

MRS. BENNET. (*Pleading.*) Lizzie?

(ELIZABETH *grimly goes to the piano and begins playing the song again.*)

LADY CATHERINE. (*Talking as* ELIZABETH *plays.*) Not bad. Not bad at all. You know, Mrs. Bennet, that pianoforte is one of the finest instruments in the country.

MRS. BENNET. It sounds exquisite.

(COLLINS *and* CHARLOTTE *enter, accompanied by* LADY LUCAS *and* SIR WILLIAM LUCAS.)

COLLINS. (*Mumbling.*) I'm sorry we are—

CHARLOTTE. My fault, really—

LADY CATHERINE. Ah, Collins—Mrs. Collins—come in.

COLLINS. You know Sir William and Lady Lucas.

LADY CATHERINE. Your cousin was just playing for us. (*There are general introductions to* ANNE *and murmured acknowledgements by everyone, and all this time* ELIZABETH *keeps playing. She stops for a moment.*) Go right on, my dear. (ELIZABETH *starts again. To* COLLINS.) You know, Miss Elizabeth shows some signs of proficiency. Ah, me. I should have been a very proficient musician had I ever learned.

COLLINS. You would have been proficient at anything.

(DARCY *enters* U. C.)

LADY CATHERINE. And so would Anne.

COLLINS. That goes without saying. (DARCY *stops at the doorway and looks at* ELIZABETH *at the piano. She does not see him.*)

LADY CATHERINE. Darcy! There you are, I've been expecting you.

DARCY. It's good to be here, Aunt Kate.

(ELIZABETH *stops playing as she hears his voice.* DARCY *goes to his* AUNT *and embraces her. He kisses* ANNE'S *hand.*)

LADY CATHERINE. Mr. Collins—Mrs. Collins, I believe you have met my nephew, Darcy. (DARCY *doesn't hear. He is looking at* ELIZABETH. *Impatiently.*) Darcy. (DARCY *comes to and turns to them.*)

COLLINS. Yes, we have had the honor of meeting Mr. Darcy. And you know Sir William—

LADY CATHERINE. (*To* DARCY.) You also know Mrs. Bennet.

DARCY. A pleasure to see you again, Mrs. Bennet.

MRS. BENNET. The pleasure is all mine.

LADY CATHERINE. And Miss Elizabeth.

DARCY. (*Bowing.*) Miss Elizabeth. (*Crosses L. to between* LADY CATHERINE *and* ELIZABETH.)

ELIZABETH. (*Coolly.*) Mr. Darcy.

LADY CATHERINE. Miss Bennet was playing for us when you came in. (DARCY *turns to* LADY CATHERINE.) Do go on, Miss Bennet. (ELIZABETH *continues playing.*) You know, Darcy, I was just telling Collins, go right on, my dear, how exquisitely dear Anne would have played, if her health had permitted her to study. (DARCY *is not listening. He is looking at* ELIZABETH. *Addressing the others.*) Darcy's dear mother was so fond of Anne.

COLLINS. Who wouldn't be fond of Anne, eh, Mrs. Bennet?

MRS. BENNET. Who, indeed?

(DARCY *crosses L. above piano, watches* ELIZABETH.)

LADY CATHERINE. She used to say to me, "Kate, you have an only daughter and I have an only son. It's as though Providence had created them for one another," she used to say. Remember that, Darcy? (DARCY *is paying no attention. Impatiently.*) Darcy.

DARCY. (*He turns back to her.*) Yes. Lovely, lovely. (*Crosses U. L. of piano.*)

LADY CATHERINE. (*A little annoyed.*) Miss Elizabeth, I don't know that piece. What is it?

DARCY. (*Before* ELIZABETH *has a chance to answer.*) It's called "Love Will Find Out the Way."

LADY CATHERINE. How did you know?

DARCY. Miss Bennet has played it for me before.

LADY CATHERINE. Oh. (*After a moment she applauds politely.*) Well, thank you, Miss Elizabeth. That was very nice. Very nice, indeed. (ELIZABETH *stops playing.*)

DARCY. Oh, I'm sorry you stopped. That was charming.

ELIZABETH. That is the right time to stop . . . when people still think you are charming. If I went on, you might change your mind. As you have before.

DARCY. A man may change his mind many times about many things. It's good to see you again, Miss Elizabeth.

ELIZABETH. I thought you were staying in London, Mr. Darcy.

DARCY. Well, I—uh—uh—left there this morning. Rather unexpectedly, as a matter of fact.

ELIZABETH. All your departures seem to be rather unexpected, Mr. Darcy.

(*The* OTHERS, *especially* LADY CATHERINE, *are listening to this conversation.* LADY CATHERINE *decides to break it up.*)

LADY CATHERINE. Miss Elizabeth, come here. (ELIZABETH

goes o ther.) Your playing is quite creditable, my dear. You know, you wouldn't play at all badly if you practiced more. Practice, Miss Elizabeth, practice. You can't do enough of it. The Collinses have no piano, of course, but you are very welcome to practice here at any time during your stay.

MRS. BENNET. Isn't that lovely!

ELIZABETH. Thank you, Lady Catherine.

LADY CATHERINE. There is quite a good instrument in the housekeeper's room. If you play there you will disturb no one.

ELIZABETH. You are really too gracious, Lady Catherine. But I should not care to disturb the housekeeper.

(LADY CATHERINE *rises, is beginning to swell up like a balloon.* ELIZABETH *is breathing deeply, trying to keep her temper.*)

DARCY. (*Jumping in.*) Now, now, Aunt Kate. Why all this talk of practicing when Miss Bennet should be playing? (*To* ELIZABETH.) Miss Elizabeth, I insist on your favoring us again.

(ELIZABETH *looks at him for a moment. Now she can no longer contain herself. She starts to run Offstage. Just before going off, she stops, turns to* LADY CATHERINE.)

ELIZABETH. (*On the verge of tears.*) Lady Catherine, may I be excused? I would like a breath of air.

LADY CATHERINE. (*Coldly.*) Lunch will be served very shortly and— (ELIZABETH *goes without waiting for* LADY CATHERINE *to finish her speech. Indignant.*) Well!

COLLINS. Lady Catherine, please excuse this intolerable breach. The girl has never been taught any better.

MRS. BENNET. Mr. Collins!

DARCY. I think she was offended.

LADY CATHERINE. Offended? Well, certainly not by me. You know I am the soul of tact.

MRS. BENNET. She was upset. I know Lizzie. Perhaps I should go talk to her.

DARCY. (*Quickly.*) Let me go.

MRS. BENNET. (*Just as quickly.*) Of course. (DARCY *exits* R. *1.*)

BUTLER. (*He enters.*) Lunch is served, milady.

LADY CATHERINE. Good. (*She rises.*) We will not wait for them. Have no fondness for cold soup. Come along, come along. Collins, bring in Lady Anne.

(*She marches off, followed by* COLLINS, ANNE, CHARLOTTE *and* MRS. BENNET. MRS. BENNET *pauses at the doorway, turns, looks Offstage towards where* DARCY *and* ELIZABETH *exited.*)

Mrs. Bennet. (*Smiling.*) A house in town. (*She goes. Bows to* Butler *on exit.*)

(*Stage remains vacant for a moment. Then* Elizabeth *enters in hurried agitation. She looks about her and sees everyone is gone.* Darcy *strolls on in the manner of a man who has been following her.*)

Darcy. That was a very short breath of air you took.

Elizabeth. The air suddenly became stifling out there, too. I wish you hadn't followed me.

Darcy. I wanted to explain my aunt's behavior. Her manner is sometimes unfortunate.

Elizabeth. Mr. Darcy, having already met you, I was happily well prepared for your aunt's manner. (*She looks around her.*) I assume everyone has gone to lunch.

Darcy. It seems they didn't wait for us. (Elizabeth *starts for the doorway. She hesitates then goes to another exit.*) Lunch is on the south terrace. I will take you there after a moment.

Elizabeth. I would like to go now.

Darcy. I would like to talk to you.

Elizabeth. I do not wish to talk to you.

Darcy. I am puzzled. It seems to me that my behavior today has been impeccable. I have tried to be most friendly.

Elizabeth. Yes, you have put on a great show of friendliness and courtesy. Mr. Darcy, I don't know which I dislike more—your former rudeness, or your present hypocrisy.

Darcy. (*Pointing to a chair.*) Miss Elizabeth, please have a chair.

Elizabeth. No, thank you.

Darcy. (*Sharply.*) Sit down! Please. (*She remains standing.* Darcy *starts song "THE HEART HAS WON THE GAME."*)

MUSIC: 32

(*Verse.*)
Sometimes a man will act against his better judgment
Sometimes a man is not the master of his fate

(*Refrain.*)
Long have I tried to doubt this feeling
Hard have I fought to deny its claim
Strive though I may to play my part with caution
It's just no use
The heart has won the game

Soft are the words I long to tell you
Sweet are the thoughts when I speak your name

Strong is the urge to linger close beside you
Make no mistake
The heart has won the game

How fair the face
How fine the eyes
How warm the touch
How bright the smile

Long have I tried to turn aside this feeling
But I'm undone
My reckless heart has won
The game.

(*After song:* ELIZABETH *is stunned. She tries to speak.*)

(*Riding right over her.*) I didn't realize it until I was away from you. Elizabeth—these last weeks since I left Netherfield and you, have been empty, meaningless days and nights. I thought I could put you out of my mind—that my heart would give way to reason. I have walked the streets of London, telling myself of the unsuitability of such a marriage—of the obstacles between us—but it won't do. I can struggle against you no longer.

ELIZABETH. (*Absolutely thrown.*) Mr. Darcy, I— I—

DARCY. (*Going right on.*) I have reminded myself again and again that I have obligations of family and position—obligations that I was born to. But nothing seems to matter. Elizabeth, I want you to marry me.

ELIZABETH. (*Wryly.*) Marry you.

DARCY. (*Puzzled.*) Yes.

ELIZABETH. Mr. Darcy, if you were not so lacking in perception, you might have spared yourself my refusal.

DARCY. Is this the only reply I am to be honored with? I think I deserve to be told why I am rejected, and with so little civility.

ELIZABETH. Mr. Darcy, did you think I would swoon with delight because you have overcome your aversion to my family and are now ready to marry into it?

DARCY. Surely you didn't expect me to be happy because your family is inferior to mine? I am overlooking that fact because it is not your fault.

ELIZABETH. Thank you. I suppose I should be flattered when you tell me that you like me—love me—against your will, against your reason, even against your character.

DARCY. Miss Elizabeth, if the manner of my expression offended you—

ELIZABETH. (*Going on.*) And did you expect me to accept the man who has destroyed the happiness of my sister, the sweetest soul that ever lived? How could you do it?

DARCY. I did not believe that she really loved Charles. In my opinion, the entire affair was the result of your mother's machinations.

ELIZABETH. (*Sarcastically.*) In your opinion.

DARCY. Therefore, I considered it my duty to separate my friend from your sister. Towards him I have been kinder than towards myself.

ELIZABETH. And towards Captain Wickham?

DARCY. You take an eager interest in that gentleman's concerns.

ELIZABETH. So would anyone who knows what he has suffered at your hands.

DARCY. Where Wickham is concerned I have nothing to say.

ELIZABETH. Because you know you are guilty.

DARCY. And this is your opinion of me. I thank you for explaining it so fully. Perhaps you would have thought better of me had I been less honest. I see I have hurt your pride with my honest confession. I suppose I should have flattered you and concealed all my doubts—all my troubled feelings—but I couldn't.

ELIZABETH. Let us end this distasteful subject. Your arrogance, your conceit, your selfish disregard of other people's feelings made me dislike you from the first. I hadn't known you for a week before I decided you were—

DARCY. (*Interrupting her.*) You have said quite enough. Madam, I understand your feelings. I am only ashamed of having confessed my own. Forgive me for having taken up so much of your valuable time and accept my best wishes for your health and happiness. (*He turns and goes.*)

MUSIC: 33

ELIZABETH. (*Looking after him.*)
Am I quick to judge?
Did I go too far?
Was I wrong?
Was I wrong?

I believe in saying what I think
And I know no other way to be
I am not the dainty feminine kind
Ladylike and overrefined
I just can't help speaking my mind
I'm me
I'm me
Just me

I believe in doing what I like
Though at times the world may disagree
I've been told I ought to try to give in

But I don't know how to begin
Much to everybody's chagrin
I'm me
I'm me

Why should I care
If I'm not a maiden fair
If, alas, I'm not the lass with the delicate air
Should I care?
Should I care?

I refuse to bow before the wind
Like the fragile branches of a tree
I suppose I'm just an obstinate fool
One part woman, the other part mule
Try to make me anything else, you'll see
I will never change
I'm me.
I will never change
I'm me.

MUSIC SEGUE: 34

ACT TWO

SCENE 3

A street in Meryton. In One. We see exterior of shops, etc. The wicker traveling case is on stage. We see TWO PEOPLE *with their arms around each other. They are kissing, lost to the world. They are* LYDIA *and* WICKHAM. *They separate.*

LYDIA. Captain Wickham, this is a public street.

WICKHAM. I was carried away. I'm sorry.

LYDIA. I'm not.

WICKHAM. I should spank you and send you away, but you're too delicious.

LYDIA. I once thought it was Lizzie you wanted.

WICKHAM. Your sister is too intelligent for me. I like young idiots like you. (*They kiss again.*)

LYDIA. Oh, Wickie, I can't bear the thought of you leaving. How long will you be in Brighton?

WICKHAM. All I know is that the Regiment is being transferred. When one takes the King's shilling, one takes his orders. (*Sudden thought.*) Lydia, come with me!

LYDIA. Captain Wickham!

WICKHAM. Oh, your family.

LYDIA. Of course, I might be able to. Mother and Lizzie are still visiting Charlotte and Mr. Collins in Kent. And Papa believes anything I tell him.

WICKHAM. How long will it take you to get your things packed?

LYDIA. I've thought of that. (*She goes to wicker bag, picks it up.*) I'm already packed—I was beginning to think you'd never ask me.

WICKHAM. (*He puts his arm around her.*) You had it all planned. (*They kiss.*) What about money? I'm temporarily—

LYDIA. I've been saving. I have a little more than a little. (*She looks Offstage.*) You wait here and I'll be right back.

(*They kiss. She exits.* OFFICERS *enter as she is going.*)

FIRST OFFICER. Say, Wickham, who was the daisy?

WICKHAM. A friend.

SECOND OFFICER. Wickham, how is it that you get such pretty friends?

WICKHAM. The Wickhams have always had the prettiest friends. That honor was granted to us in the Magna Carta.

FIRST OFFICER. (*Picking up hat box.*) Does this belong to your friend?

WICKHAM. (*Reaching for the box.*) Yes.

(FIRST OFFICER *snatches it away and opens it. He pulls out a dress.*)

SECOND OFFICER. (*Sees dress, whistles.*) Is she going to Brighton with you?

(WICKHAM *just stands there with a small smile and his eyebrows lifted.*)

FIRST OFFICER. Wickham, how do you do it?

WICKHAM. It's an old family recipe. Gentlemen, you take one girl, one Wickham, and a dash of military tactics.

MUSIC: 35

(*Into DANCE. At end of Dance,* WICKHAM *exits.*)
SEGUE: 35A

BLACKOUT

FLY DROP

ACT TWO

SCENES 4 and 5

Longbourn. Interior.

MRS. BENNET *is lying on a chaise or settee.* KITTY *and* MARY *are comforting her, putting wet towels on her head, etc.*

MRS. BENNET. (*Loud moan.*) Oh, what did I ever do to deserve this? Oh, Lydia, how could you do this to me? I warned her— (*Rises and crosses slowly* R., *assisted by* MARY.) "Beware of officers, Lydia," I said. "They are wicked, immoral, and worst of all, they never have a sixpence."

KITTY. (*Crosses* D. L. *of sofa.*) I still think officers are nice.

MRS. BENNET. (*Indignant.*) If I had my way, all officers would be abolished. (*Crosses back* L., *sits on sofa.*)

KITTY. (*Sits sofa.*) But, Mother, if they abolish officers who would run the army?

MRS. BENNET. Generals.

MARY. Generals are officers.

MRS. BENNET. But they're too old to do any harm. My lovely, darling, gentle little Lydia—

KITTY. Mama! Mama!

(JANE *enters* L. *1 with bowl of soup. Crosses to sofa.*)

MRS. BENNET. What's that you're bringing me, food? Take it away.

JANE. Mother, it's delicious chicken broth.

MRS. BENNET. You know I'm too ill to eat. (JANE *starts out* R.) Did you say chicken broth? Well, perhaps if I made a great effort. (KITTY *moves back above sofa.* JANE *crosses to sofa, sits.* MRS. BENNET *takes soup bowl. Sitting up and looking at the bowl of broth.*) Why are there no dumplings? (JANE *just looks at her and starts feeding her broth with a spoon.*) Well, I doubt if I could get a dumpling down. (*Looks around the room.*) Where's Lizzie?

JANE. She's gone to meet Papa.

MRS. BENNET. Oh, yes.

KITTY. Maybe Papa will have some good news.

JANE. I'm sure they are hiding some place in London, Mama. After all, they were seen there. Papa will find them.

MARY. Maybe he'll challenge Captain Wickham to a duel.

MRS. BENNET. And get himself killed! Then what will become of us? Those Collinses will turn us out before your father is cold in his grave.

MAID. (*Enters* R. *1.*) Mr. and Mrs. Collins have just driven up. (*Crosses* R. *1.*)

MRS. BENNET. Oh! The vultures! They're here already.

JANE. (*Whispering.*) Please, Mama.

MRS. BENNET. Don't worry, they shan't have the satisfaction of seeing me suffer.

(COLLINS *and* CHARLOTTE *enter* R. *1, cross to* C. JANE *crosses* L., *puts soup bowl on desk.*)

CHARLOTTE. Mrs. Bennet, we came just as soon as we heard the news. It's so dreadful.

MRS. BENNET. (*Brightly.*) Now, now, Charlotte, it's not that serious. (*She collapses in tears.* CHARLOTTE *and* COLLINS *cross each other.*)

COLLINS. Mrs. Bennet, dear cousin, we're here to bring you what little comfort we can. May I say that from what I've heard, your daughter Lydia would be better off dead.

CHARLOTTE. Mr. Collins!

COLLINS. (*Crosses* D. R. *to* CHARLOTTE.) I was trying to bring Mrs. Bennet some consolation.

(ELIZABETH *enters with* MR. BENNET U. C. *Crosses to sofa.*)

ELIZABETH. Mama, we have news. At least Papa has.

MRS. BENNET. What is it? How is my child?

MR. BENNET. When I arrived back here in Meryton, there was a letter waiting for me at the Post House. (*He takes letter from his breast pocket.*)

ELIZABETH. It sounds like good news, Mama.

MRS. BENNET. Good news?

ELIZABETH. Well, it may not be really good news, but I think he's going to marry Lydia.

MRS. BENNET. I told you he was a gentleman!

MR. BENNET. I don't understand it. Wickham is in debt. He's a gambler. And suddenly he's willing to marry a girl like Lydia and asks only for her pathetic little dowry.

ELIZABETH. The letter says that Captain Wickham has recently come into a very considerable sum of money.

MR. BENNET. (*Puzzled.*) I still do not understand—

MAID. (*Enters in a hurry. Flustered.*) It's Lady Catherine de Bourgh.

(LADY CATHERINE *enters.*)

COLLINS. Your Ladyship! What an honor for this humble house.

LADY CATHERINE. No honor was intended, Mr. Collins.

MRS. BENNET. Lady Catherine, I never expected to see you here.

LADY CATHERINE. And you were quite right. (*Looks at* MR. BENNET.) You, I presume, are Mr. Bennet?

MR. BENNET. (*Slight bow.*) I am, Your Ladyship.

LADY CATHERINE. (*Startled.*) You appear to be a gentleman!

MR. BENNET. A fallen gentleman, Your Ladyship. I was forced to abandon my class because I had no stomach for rudeness. If you will excuse me. (*He goes.*)

COLLINS. (*Rises, calls.*) Mr. Bennet, you are talking to Lady Catherine.

LADY CATHERINE. Never mind, Collins. He has wit. (COLLINS *giggles.*)

MRS. BENNET. You must excuse us all, Lady Catherine. We've had a very trying week.

LADY CATHERINE. I know. Your daughter ran off with a scoundrel. Which she never would have done had she been raised properly.

MRS. BENNET. Lady Catherine, by all the laws of noblesse oblige—

COLLINS. (*Agitatedly cutting in.*) Oh, dear! You mustn't—

ELIZABETH. (*Stopping everyone.*) One moment! Lady Catherine, to what do we owe the honor of this visit?

LADY CATHERINE. I came to see you. Alone. I'd like everyone else to go elsewhere. If there is an elsewhere in this house.

ELIZABETH. I don't know if I care to be alone with you under these—

COLLINS. Miss Elizabeth!

MRS. BENNET. Now, Lizzie, Lady Catherine wishes to speak with you, and I think we should all— Out, out, everyone, out.

COLLINS. Yes, come along. Lady Catherine wants to be alone with Miss Elizabeth. (*He claps his hands.*) Come, come.

MRS. BENNET. Lady Catherine, I hope we shall have the pleasure of seeing you later.

LADY CATHERINE. I doubt it.

COLLINS. She doubts it. Come along. (*Exits* L.)

MRS. BENNET. That's too bad. I wanted to show you our housekeeper's room.

(*They* ALL *go off* D. L. LADY CATHERINE *paces the room.* ELIZABETH *waits for her to speak.*)

ELIZABETH. Won't you be seated, Lady Catherine?

LADY CATHERINE. I never sit down when I have something unpleasant to say. Miss Bennet, I have just heard something which cannot possibly be true. It has been reported to me that my nephew, my own nephew, Mr. Darcy, fancies himself in love with you. I know this is impossible. Nevertheless, I resolved to come and speak with you about it.

ELIZABETH. If you know it's impossible, why make this long journey?

LADY CATHERINE. I came here to see to it that this vicious rumor is universally contradicted.

ELIZABETH. It seems to me that your coming here would confirm it.

LADY CATHERINE. Don't be impertinent, Miss Bennet. I am not as easy-going as I appear to be. Tell me, has my nephew made you an offer of marriage?

ELIZABETH. From what you say, that would be impossible, wouldn't it?

LADY CATHERINE. It certainly would, because I have the power to make it impossible. Marry him and you both will be cut off from every member of his class—you can never set foot in my house again.

ELIZABETH. That would be no tragedy for me, Lady Catherine.

LADY CATHERINE. Are you engaged to him?

ELIZABETH. I am not.

LADY CATHERINE. And will you promise me never to enter into such an engagement?

ELIZABETH. I will not.

LADY CATHERINE. Aha! So you do expect him to propose to you?

ELIZABETH. I expect nothing.

LADY CATHERINE. Then why is he at Netherfield?

ELIZABETH. (*Startled, rises.*) Netherfield? I have no idea—

LADY CATHERINE. Come now, Miss Bennet, I am not a child. Darcy is in love with you, isn't he?

ELIZABETH. I don't think he could be—not now.

LADY CATHERINE. Only a man in love could have done what he did for your family. (ELIZABETH *looks at her.*) Scouring the street and alleys of London, looking for that rascal Wickham and your silly sister.

ELIZABETH. But why would he—?

LADY CATHERINE. That's what I am here to find out. You know, Miss Bennet, a casual stranger would not have arranged for Wickham to marry your sister. Believe me, only a man in love would—

ELIZABETH. (*Shattered.*) Please, Lady Catherine. (*Sits.*)

LADY CATHERINE. You are in love with him, aren't you?

ELIZABETH. Yes, I am. But it need give you no cause for alarm. I am certain I will never see him again.

LADY CATHERINE. I don't think I believe you.

MUSIC: 36

(*We hear coachmen's TRUMPETS in the distance.* KITTY, *fol-*

lowed by MARY, *comes dashing into the room from* L., *followed by* JANE, CHARLOTTE, COLLINS *and* MRS. BENNET.)

KITTY. It's Lydia! (*She runs off* R.)

MARY. Lydia's come home! In a coach! (*She follows* KITTY *off* R. JANE *goes hurrying across the Stage past* LADY CATHERINE. COLLINS *and* CHARLOTTE *come running across.*)

MRS. BENNET. Lydia! My Lydia! (*She goes* R.)

CHARLOTTE. Lydia's back!

COLLINS. It's Lydia! (*They go* R.)

ELIZABETH. Excuse me, Lady Catherine. It's Lydia.

LADY CATHERINE. (*Caught up in the excitement.*) Lydia! It's Lydia! (*She starts off* R., *stops.*) What the devil do I care about Lydia?

DIM OUT AND CLOSE IN

ACT TWO

SCENE 6

Longbourn exterior.

LYDIA *and* WICKHAM *enter* L. *on Rise. The* BENNET FAMILY *enters* R.

LYDIA. (*Crosses* R. C. *to* MRS. BENNET, *embrace, then crosses to* R. *of her.*) Hello, Mama—Kitty—Lizzie—Papa—everyone, look! (*She points to ring on her finger.*)

MARY. It's a wedding ring. She's married.

MRS. BENNET. I'm a mother-in-law! At last! Oh, my darling. (*She embraces* LYDIA. *All the* GIRLS *join her.*) And a hug for you, too, my dear, dear son-in-law. (*She embraces* WICKHAM.)

WICKHAM. Mrs. Bennet.

MRS. BENNET. Please call me Mother. I've never been called that by a male person.

WICKHAM. Very well, Mother.

LYDIA. Mama, did you notice the carriage? It's ours. And this ring. We're rich. (*Shows ring.*)

MRS. BENNET. (*Embracing her.*) Rich! Rich. Oh, my darling child. Rich! Did you hear, Mr. Bennet, they're rich.

MR. BENNET. Yes, Mrs. Bennet, I heard.

LYDIA. Papa, you haven't congratulated us yet.

MR. BENNET. I'm sorry, my dear. (*He kisses her gently, almost in sorrow.*) Congratulations, Lydia. (*Turns to* WICKHAM.) And to you, sir. (*He turns and goes.*)

LYDIA. Never mind Papa, Wickie, he'll come round. He'll be proud of you—as I am.

MRS. BENNET. And I. Any man who can get rich so quickly—

ELIZABETH. That interests me, Captain Wickham. How did it happen? (*Crosses R. C. to* WICKHAM.)

WICKHAM. Well, it was quite a surprise. One of my—my uncles died.

MRS. BENNET. How nice.

WICKHAM. It was an uncle I hadn't seen since—uh—childhood. He'd been living in Jamaica—yes, Jamaica.

ELIZABETH. And he left you a fortune.

WICKHAM. Oh, not a fortune—a modest competence. But its coming was very timely.

ELIZABETH. Very timely, indeed. (*Crosses D. L.*)

MRS. BENNET. (*Leaping in.*) Lydia, why don't you and George go and unpack?

KITTY. First, Lydia, come and see the cook. I know she is dying to see your new husband.

MARY. And the ring.

LYDIA. Come, George, we'll give the lower classes a treat.

WICKHAM. You'll excuse me?

ELIZABETH. (*Coolly.*) With pleasure. (WICKHAM *goes.*)

MRS. BENNET. (*Crosses D. L. to* ELIZABETH.) Elizabeth Bennet, what is the meaning of all this? You were questioning Captain Wickham as if he were a highwayman. (ELIZABETH *just looks at her.*) You were very rude.

ELIZABETH. No Mother, I wasn't really rude to Wickham. I saved all my rudeness, all my cruelty for a good man. (*Crosses D. R. C.*)

MRS. BENNET. Who? (ELIZABETH *looks at her in misery.*) Mr. Darcy?

ELIZABETH. Mother, where do you think Wickham got that little financial windfall?

MRS. BENNET. He told us. From his uncle. It did sound odd, didn't it?

ELIZABETH. Mr. Darcy did it.

MRS. BENNET. (*Delighted.*) All out of love for you.

ELIZABETH. No, Mama. He did it out of human decency. I have always been wrong about him. Now I'm lost.

MRS. BENNET. Lizzie, where is Mr. Darcy now?

ELIZABETH. He's at Netherfield.

MRS. BENNET. (*Crosses R., to* ELIZABETH.) At Netherfield? Well then, let's fetch the carriage and you can go over and—

ELIZABETH. (*Stopping her.*) No, I couldn't.

MRS. BENNET. Lizzie, let me get the carriage. (ELIZABETH *shakes her head. Thinking.*) Lizzie—Lizzie, I would like to ask you a hypothetical question. Suppose there is a mother and she has a daughter—an intelligent daughter. Probably more intelligent than herself. (ELIZABETH *looks at her*. MRS. BENNET *goes on*.) Suppose this daughter had found the great love of her life—a proud man who loves her. But her own pride keeps her from him. What—what would you say to this daughter?

ELIZABETH. I would tell her to go away. (*Turns away*.)

MRS. BENNET. And that would make her happy?

ELIZABETH. (*Suddenly*.) No, it wouldn't. I would tell her to go to him—say how wrong she was—ask for his understanding and—

MUSIC: 37

(*Stops suddenly, looks at her mother. They* BOTH *sing "LET'S FETCH THE CARRIAGE."*)

ELIZABETH *and* MRS. BENNET.
    Let's fetch the carriage
    Get the tandem from the stall
    Let's fetch the carriage
    And pay a social call
    Let's hitch the harness
    Let the happy trip begin
    Let's drive up smiling
    And say we just popped in
ELIZABETH.
    I'll smile as I greet him
    And take his hand
MRS. BENNET.
    Then you'll go for a stroll
    On the grounds
ELIZABETH.
    He's a man who has character
    Charm and wit
MRS. BENNET.
    And of course he's a man
    Who has twelve thousand pounds.
ELIZABETH.
    Mother!
ELIZABETH *and* MRS. BENNET.
    Let's fetch the carriage
    There's no time to waste at all.
    Let's fetch the carriage
    And pay a sociable social call.

    Swift smart and stylish
    Like the London coach express
    Let's hope the journey
    Will meet with great success

MRS. BENNET.
    Now when he proposes you must be sweet
ELIZABETH.
    Well I think I'm no longer inept
MRS. BENNET.
    Be sure to be eager, be quick, be glad
ELIZABETH.
    Most important of all I'll be sure to accept.
BOTH.
    Let's fetch the carriage
    There's no time to waste at all
    Let's fetch the carriage and pay. . . .

(ELIZABETH *stops singing on the word "fetch" and* MRS. BENNET
continues until ELIZABETH *stops her with "But Mama."*)

ELIZABETH. But, Mama, what if—?
MRS. BENNET. What if what?
ELIZABETH. What if he won't have me?
MRS. BENNET. (*Indignant.*) Won't have you? After you have
gone to him on your hands and knees. He can't be so rude. What
about me, my hopes, my plans, my dreams, my— (*She sings
phrase.*) "house in town, a house in town." . . .
ELIZABETH. Your house in town— (*Stopping her.*) Mama,
please! It's my happiness that's involved here. I love him.
MRS. BENNET. And my mother's heart tells me he loves you,
too.

MUSIC: 37A

(Song: "LET'S FETCH THE CARRIAGE.")

MRS. BENNET.
    Let's plan a marriage today
    For early
ELIZABETH.
    Fall—in love,
    Says my mother take him or any other
ELIZABETH *and* MRS. BENNET.
    Let's fetch the carriage
    And pay a sociable call.

(*There is a CLAP OF THUNDER heard.*)

ELIZABETH.
    Mama!
                (*THUNDER.*)
    Mama, never mind the carriage. I'll use the horse.

MRS. BENNET.
Good girl.

BLACKOUT

ACT TWO

SCENE 7

Netherfield Hall. Garden, in depth.

Night time, immediately afterwards. BINGLEY *is alone.* DARCY
enters U. R.

DARCY. (*Impatient.*) Bingley, we have many things to do if
we are going to leave.

BINGLEY. The rain has stopped.

DARCY. I would like to get away from here. I thought we were
going to close the place up and leave as soon as possible.

BINGLEY. (*Paying no attention.*) I remember it was a night
like this when Jane first came to Netherfield. Maybe I should go
to see her. Oh, I know you're against it and Caroline's against it.

DARCY. If you want to humble yourself and be made to feel a
fool— (*Sudden recovery.*) Charles, you are your own master.

(LADY CATHERINE'S VOICE *is heard Offstage.*)

LADY CATHERINE. (*Enters from* R.) Darcy, ah, there you are.
I've been looking all over for you.

DARCY. Aunt Kate, what are you doing at Netherfield?

LADY CATHERINE. I came here directly from the Bennets.

DARCY. The Bennets?

BINGLEY. Lady Catherine, did you see Miss Jane? Miss Jane
Bennet? A beautiful girl.

LADY CATHERINE. Charles, what is she to you?

BINGLEY. I'm going to find out. (*He exits* R.)

LADY CATHERINE. (*Looking after him.*) Those Bennets must
practice witchcraft.

DARCY. (*Slightly menacing.*) Aunt Kate, why did you visit the
Bennets?

LADY CATHERINE. To speak to Miss Elizabeth. I felt it my
duty.

DARCY. (*Angrily.*) You had no right. (ELIZABETH *enters* R. 2.)

LADY CATHERINE. Oh, I knew you would be angry with me.
But I felt it my duty to keep the halls of Pemberley from being
polluted by someone who is only after your money and your
position.

DARCY. (*Sees* ELIZABETH *enter behind* LADY CATHERINE.) Aunt Kate, I don't wish to discuss Miss Bennet. (*He looks at* ELIZABETH.) She and I will not be seeing each other again.

LADY CATHERINE. Well, I'm glad I helped you come to your senses. I did not look on this match with a friendly eye. (*She notices him looking past her. She looks around, sees* ELIZABETH.) She must have flown here!

DARCY. Aunt Kate. (DARCY *has crossed to* ELIZABETH.)

LADY CATHERINE. Darcy! Be careful. (*She goes.*)

ELIZABETH. I rode through the woods so I could get here quickly.

DARCY. I can think of no reason why you should want to get here quickly.

ELIZABETH. I—I wanted to thank you for what you did for Lydia.

DARCY. (*A quick look after* LADY CATHERINE.) I'm sorry my aunt told you.

ELIZABETH. I'm glad she did. It was very generous—noble of you.

DARCY. I make no claim to these qualities. I did what I did because I understood the pain you were suffering. You see, when my sister met Wickham she was even younger than Lydia.

ELIZABETH. (*Shocked.*) Your sister.

DARCY. Yes. He planned to run off with her. Then by threatening to publish her disgrace he would get a large financial settlement from me and my consent to their marriage.

ELIZABETH. How horrible.

DARCY. I discovered the plot in time and earned his eternal hatred, which I welcome. So my sister was saved. And as for your sister, her reputation is saved. So, everything has come out all right.

ELIZABETH. (*Sadly.*) Yes, everything. Well, thank you very much.

DARCY. I was happy to do it.

ELIZABETH. I had better be getting back home now.

DARCY. (*Nodding.*) Yes. You have a long ride.

ELIZABETH. Well, good-bye.

DARCY. Good-bye. This is perhaps the last time we shall meet. God bless you, Elizabeth.

MUSIC: 38

(*He turns.* ELIZABETH *sings reprise of "THE HEART HAS WON THE GAME" with her lyrics.*)

(*Verse.*)
Sometimes a girl will act against better judgment
Sometimes she cannot be mistress of her fate

(*Refrain.*)

Long have I tried to doubt this feeling
Hard have I fought to deny its claim
Strive though I may to play my part with caution
It's just no use
The heart has won the game.

DARCY. (*Spoken.*)
How fair the face
How fine the eyes
How warm the touch
How bright the smile

Long have I tried to turn aside this feeling
But I'm undone
My reckless heart has won
The game.

ACT TWO

SCENE 8

MUSIC: 39

SEGUE: 39A

DIM UP on garden at Netherfield. PEOPLE *enter from L. and R., begin to dance.* KITTY *and* MARY *enter from L., cross to R.* LT. DENNY *and* LT. ROCKINGHAM *enter from R., start across L., pass the* GIRLS.

KITTY. Mary!

(MARY, *going off R., stops, turns. They begin to dance.* BINGLEY *and* JANE *enter.*)

BINGLEY. Jane, your sister's cold is much better.
JANE. Oh, I knew Lizzie would be all right once she and Mr. Darcy— I mean, she couldn't very well miss a party that is given in her honor.
BINGLEY. And yours. However, I do think it's time your mother stopped arranging colds for her daughters in order to catch us poor souls.
DARCY. (*He has entered from R.*) Elizabeth arranged this cold herself. (*DANCE cue.* ELIZABETH *enters R.* DARCY *hurries to her.*) Elizabeth—here, let me get you a chair.
ELIZABETH. No, I'd like to dance.
DARCY. Are you sure you should?
ELIZABETH. Oh, yes.

DARCY. But your cold.

ELIZABETH. Mr. Darcy, may I please have the honor of this dance with you?

DARCY. Miss Elizabeth, I'm afraid the honor of dancing with you is more than I can bear.

(*They smile, start dancing.* MRS. BENNET *enters* U. R. *with* MR. BENNET, *eavesdrops on following dialogue.* WICKHAM *and* LYDIA *dance their way* D. L.)

WICKHAM. So now I'm to be Darcy's relative.

LYDIA. I told you I was a catch, Wickie.

BINGLEY. Jane—

JANE. Yes, Charles?

BINGLEY. Nothing. Just Jane.

MARY. I haven't seen you for quite a while.

LT. DENNY. I've been away studying for my new position in the army.

MARY. Your new position? What is it?

LT. DENNY. I'm a bugler.

MARY. How wonderful—a musician!

KITTY. My name is Kitty.

LT. ROCKINGHAM. My name is Tom.

KITTY. Isn't that a coincidence!

MRS. BENNET. Mr. Darcy?

DARCY. Yes, Mrs. Bennet.

MRS. BENNET. Mr. Darcy, I was thinking. You and Elizabeth— when you are married, will you be living in London?

ELIZABETH. Oh, no, Mama. I'm looking forward to Pe berley. I know it's beautiful, and I do not want to live in London.

(MINUET)   *MUSIC: 40*

MRS. BENNET. But you do have a house in London. Who will be using it while you're in Pemberley?

DARCY. Well— (*To* ELIZABETH *as they dance around.*) Why don't I let your mother have the house in London?

ELIZABETH. That would be very kind of you, but you shouldn't do it.

DARCY. My dear, let us not forget that London is over a hundred miles from Pemberley.

ELIZABETH. (*Momentarily suspicious.*) Are you still trying to get rid of my family?

DARCY. (*Very warmly.*) I'm just trying to be alone with you.

MUSIC STOPS

ELIZABETH. (*She looks at him, then turns to her* MOTHER.) Mama! (EVERYONE *stops*.) Your dream has come true.

MRS. BENNET. My house in town! (LADY LUCAS *enters* R., MR. BENNET *behind her*. MRS. BENNET *crosses to* LADY LUCAS.) Lady Lucas, you really must come and visit me at my home in London.

(LADY LUCAS *looks stunned, exits*. MRS. BENNET *crosses* R. *to* MR. BENNET. *They embrace*.)

MUSIC: 41

(ELIZABETH *sings:* "*LOVE WILL FIND OUT THE WAY*.")

CURTAIN

BOWS: MUSIC: 42

FIRST IMPRESSIONS

PROPERTY PLOT

ACT ONE

Scene 1

Longbourn Interior

At rise:
Large armchair (DR)
Harp (URC)
Straight chair (at harp)
2 straight chairs (flanking US French doors)
Chaise-sofa (DSC)
Small table (DL)
Small armchair (R of table)
Straight chair (L of table)

Hand props set at rise:
Writing paper
Quill
Deck of cards   } On table
2 hands, 5 cards each, dealt
Book (Large armchair)

Hand props off stage:
Right
Embroidery (Kitty)
Knitting (Jane)
Book (Elizabeth)
Salver w/letter (Margaret, maid)
Left
Nothing

ACT ONE

Scene 2

Country Road

At rise:
Nothing
Hand props offstage:
Right
Hatbox (Mrs. Bennet)
Hatbox (Lady Lucas)
Left
Hedge clippers (Mr. Bennet)
Whip (1st Coachman)
Posthorn (2nd Coachman)

PROPERTY PLOT

ACT ONE
Scene 3
The Assembly

At rise:

2 straight chairs (back to back) (DL)
Straight chair (DR)

Hand props off stage:

Left

Small table, w/punch bowl & dipper (liquid painted)
5 cups (Matthews butler)

ACT ONE
Scene 4
Longbourn Exterior

At rise:

Bench (for 4) (DL)

Hand props offstage:

Right

Hedge clippers (Mr. Bennet)

ACT ONE
Scene 5
Netherfield Interior

At rise:

Grand piano (not practical) (DL)
2 straight chairs (DS of piano)
Piano bench (at piano)
Billiard table, w/cuestick, and 3 balls set in triangle (C)
Secretary, w/writing paper, quill, inkstand, small box containing
   playing cards, shelves filled with books (DR)
Small armchair (at secretary)
Straight chair (US of secretary)
Folding cardtable (UL)
4 vases on stands (against walls UL, ULC, UC, R)
Hanging chandelier, 2 lamps (not practical) (C)

Offstage Hand props:

Right

Packet of letters (Miss Bingley)
Suitcase (Elizabeth)

OFFSTAGE PRACTICAL PIANO & STOOL: LEFT

ACT ONE
Scene 6
Longbourn Exterior

At rise:

Same as 1-4 (Bench)

Hand props offstage:

Same as 1-4 (Clippers R)

ACT ONE
Scene 7
Netherfield Exterior

At rise:
Hedge mazes
2 small standing umbrellas, w/poles (DL & DR)
Large standing umbrella, w/pole on large oval seat (C)
Archery bow, quiver w/4 arrows (DL Proscenium)
Archery target (trick arrow fixed in bullseye)
  (DR Proscenium)
Rolling tea cart, holding punch bowl & dipper (liquid painted)
  and 3 cups (chorus dancer)

ACT ONE
Scene 8
Netherfield Exterior (in one)

At rise:
Bow, arrows, quiver, and target remain from 1-7

ACT ONE
Scene 9
Longbourn Interior

At rise:
Furniture set-up exactly as in L-1
Hand props off stage:
Book (Large armchair)
Hand props off stage:
Left
Letter (Lydia)

ACT TWO
Scene 1
Church in Kent

At rise:
Nothing
Hand props off stage:
Right
Wedding bouquet (Charlotte)

ACT TWO
Scene 2
Rosings

At rise:
Straight chair (DR)
Love seat (R)
Throne-like armchair (C)
Piano (not practical) (DL)
Piano stool (at piano)

Light straight chair (below piano)
Painting of Lord deBourgh (hanging UC)
Painting of Lady Catherine (hanging R)
Painting of Darcy as boy (hanging L)
  Hand props off stage:
Right
Cane (Lady Catherine)
Left
Book (Elizabeth)
OFFSTAGE PRACTICAL PIANO & STOOL: Left

ACT TWO
Scene 3
Meryton Street

  At rise:

Large hatbox-like suitcase w/removable cover, containing break-
  away dress (bodice, skirt, 2 sleeves)
  Offstage hand props:
Left
Half-slip (handed to chorus dancer)

ACT TWO
Scene 4
Longbourn Interior

  At rise:

Furniture set-up exactly as in I-1 (sofa raked less)
  Offstage hand props:
Right
Letter (Mr. Bennet)
Cane (Lady Catherine)
Left
Tray w/soup bowl & spoon (Jane)

ACT TWO
Scene 5
Longbourn Exterior

No bench
  Offstage hand props:
Left
Wedding ring (Lydia)

ACT TWO
Scene 6
Netherfield Exterior

  At rise:

Set-up exactly as in I-7 (Hedges, umbrellas)

Offstage hand props:
Right
Cane (Lady Catherine)

ACT TWO
Scene 7 (Finale)
Netherfield Exterior

At rise:
Set-up as II-6
THUNDER SHEET HANGS STAGE LEFT (Used in I-4 & II-5)

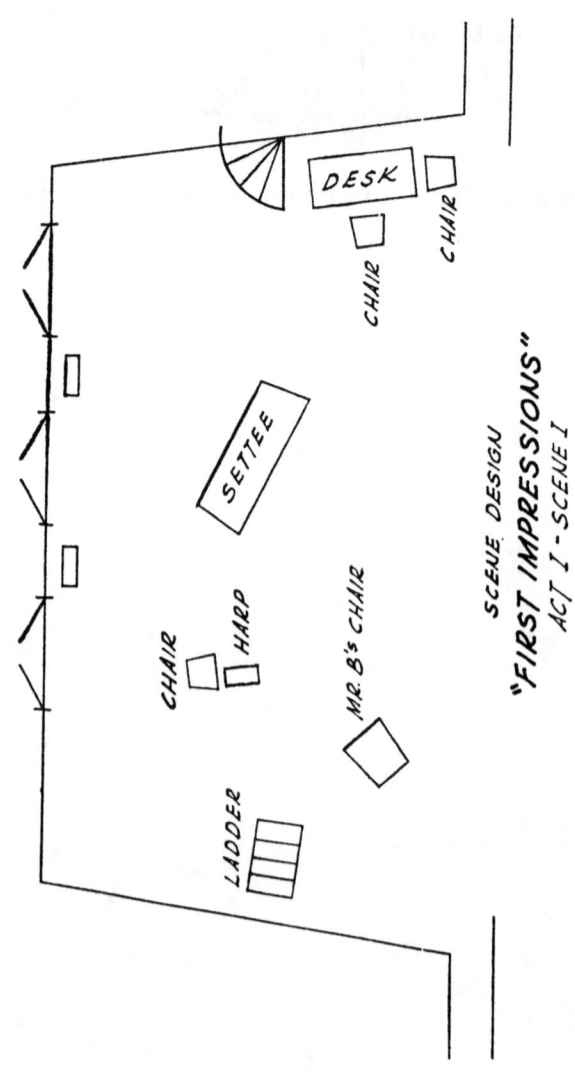

SCENE DESIGN

"FIRST IMPRESSIONS"

ACT I - SCENE I

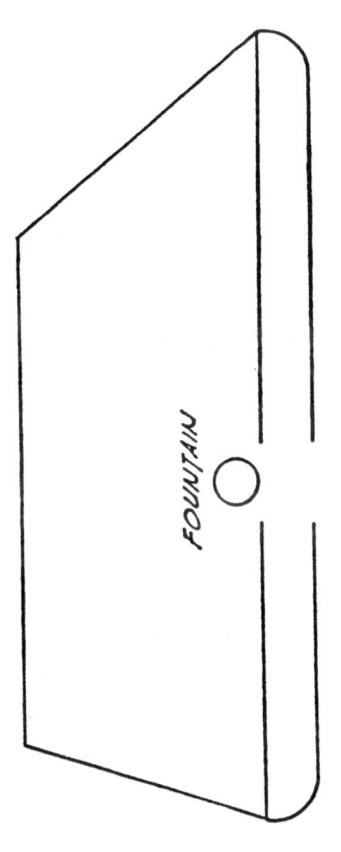

FOUNTAIN

SCENE DESIGN
"FIRST IMPRESSIONS"
ACT I · SCENE 2

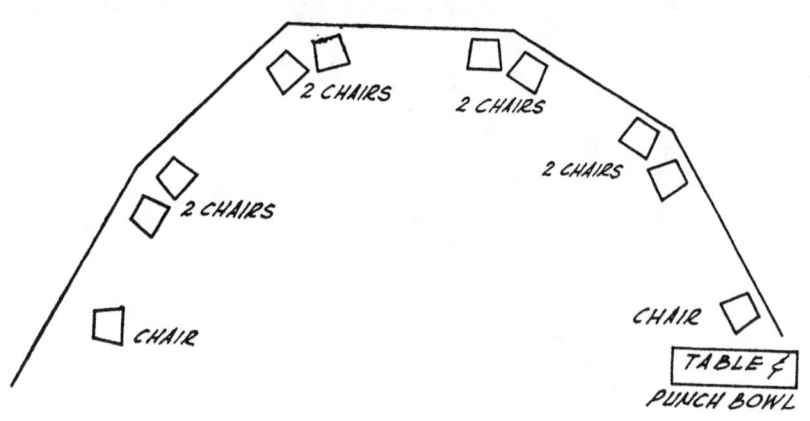

SCENE DESIGN
"FIRST IMPRESSIONS"
ACT I - SCENE 3

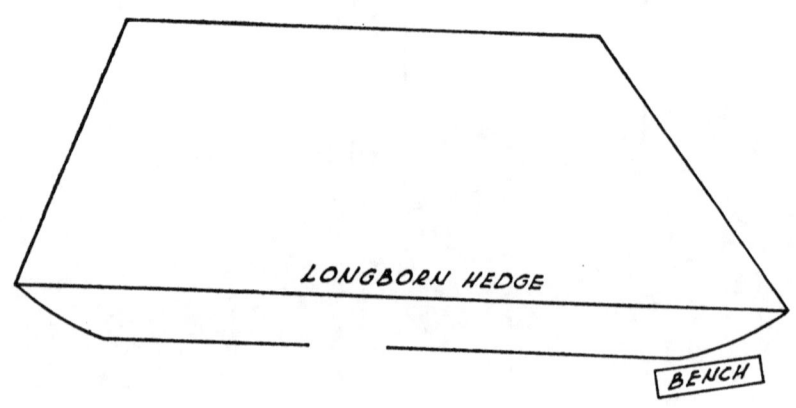

SCENE DESIGN
"FIRST IMPRESSIONS"
ACT I - SCENE 4 & SCENE 6

SCENE DESIGN
"FIRST IMPRESSIONS"
ACT 1 · SCENE 5

PIANO

CHAIR

CARD
TABLE

CHAIR

POOL TABLE

COAT RACK

STAIRS

CHAIR

CHAIR

SEC.

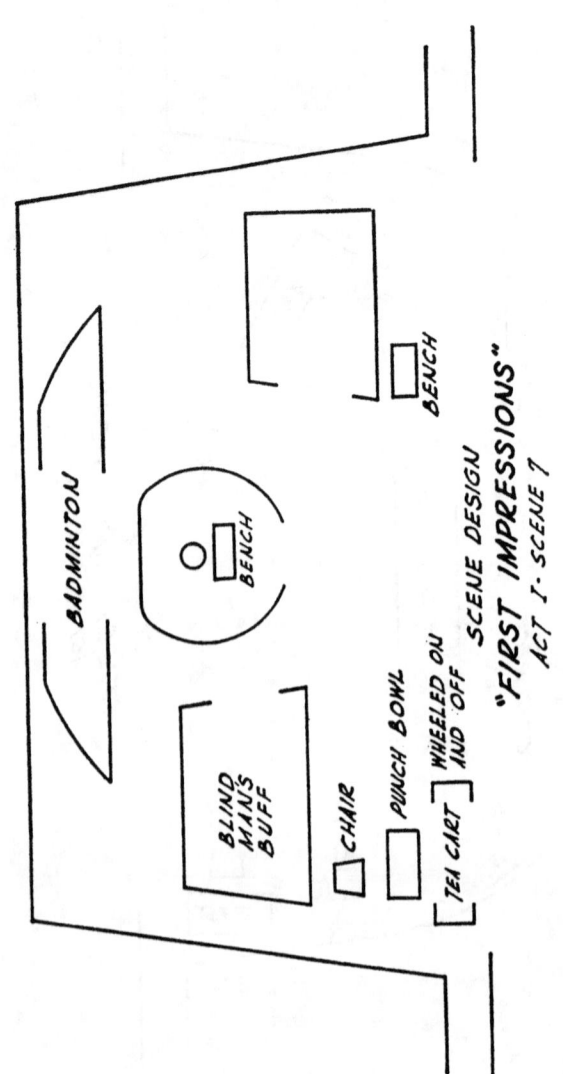

BADMINTON

BENCH

BLIND
MAN'S
BUFF

BENCH

CHAIR

PUNCH BOWL

[TEA CART]

WHEELED ON
AND OFF

SCENE DESIGN

"FIRST IMPRESSIONS"
ACT I · SCENE 1

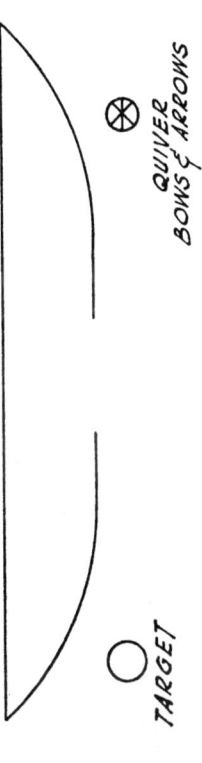

TARGET

QUIVER
BOWS & ARROWS

SCENE DESIGN
"FIRST IMPRESSIONS"
ACT I - SCENE 6

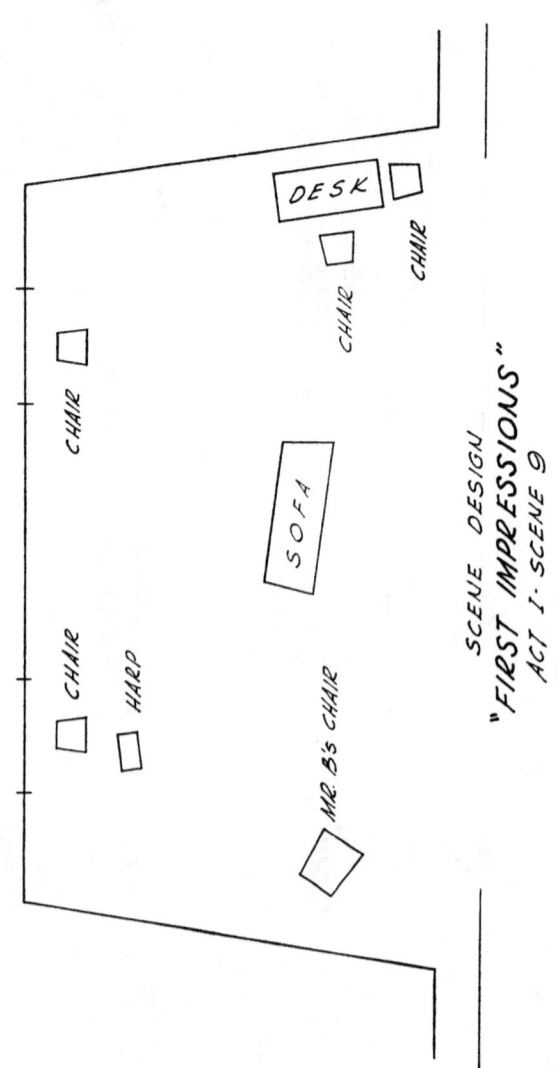

SCENE DESIGN
"FIRST IMPRESSIONS"
ACT 1· SCENE 9

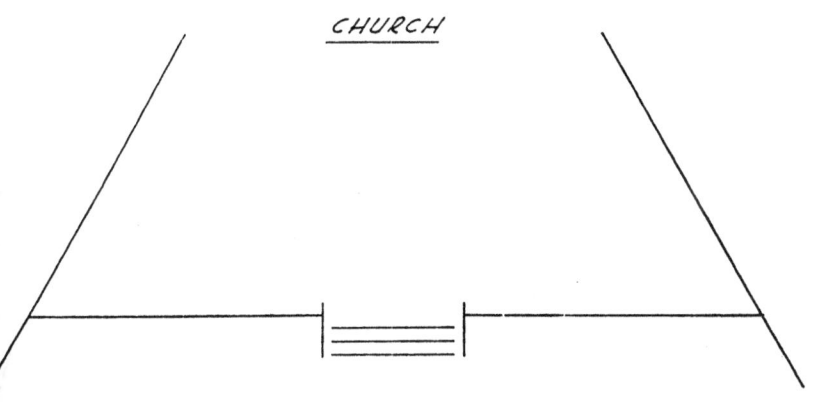

SCENE DESIGN
"FIRST IMPRESSIONS"
ACT 2 · SCENE I

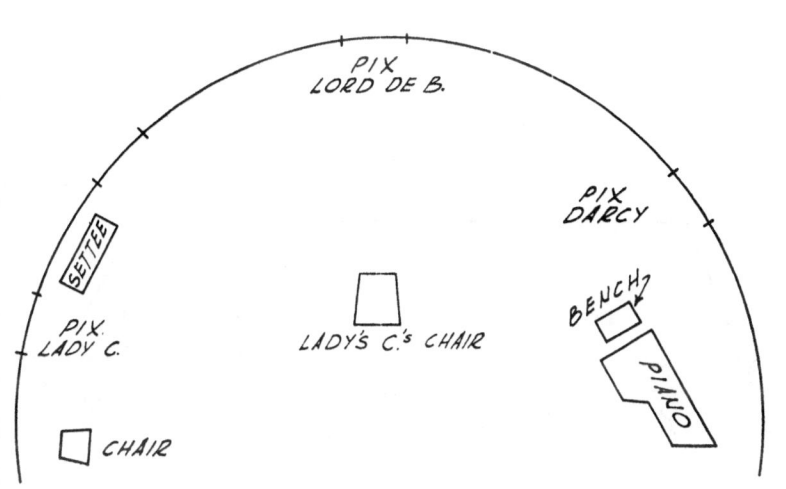

SCENE DESIGN
"FIRST IMPRESSIONS"
ACT 2 · SCENE 2

[MERYTON]

STREET DROP

SCENE DESIGN
"FIRST IMPRESSIONS"
ACT 2 - SCENE 3

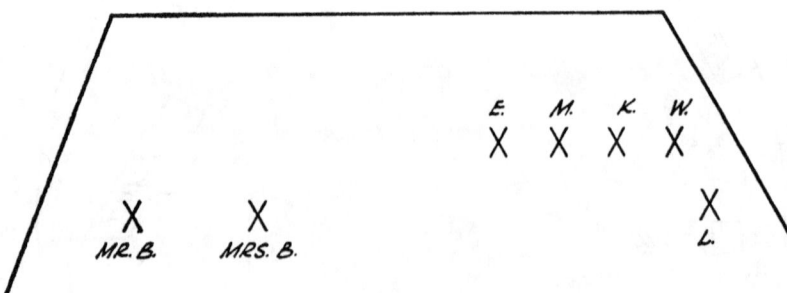

E.   M.   K.   W.
X   X   X   X

X   X   X
MR. B.   MRS. B.   L.

SCENE DESIGN
"FIRST IMPRESSIONS"
ACT 2 - SCENE 6

SKIN DEEP
Jon Lonoff

Comedy / 2m, 2f / Interior Unit Set

In *Skin Deep*, a large, lovable, lonely-heart, named Maureen Mulligan, gives romance one last shot on a blind-date with sweet awkward Joseph Spinelli; she's learned to pepper her speech with jokes to hide insecurities about her weight and appearance, while he's almost dangerously forthright, saying everything that comes to his mind. They both know they're perfect for each other, and in time they come to admit it.

They were set up on the date by Maureen's sister Sheila and her husband Squire, who are having problems of their own: Sheila undergoes a non-stop series of cosmetic surgeries to hang onto the attractive and much-desired Squire, who may or may not have long ago held designs on Maureen, who introduced him to Sheila. With Maureen particularly vulnerable to both hurting and being hurt, the time is ripe for all these unspoken issues to bubble to the surface.

"Warm-hearted comedy … the laughter was literally show-stopping. A winning play, with enough good-humored laughs and sentiment to keep you smiling from beginning to end."
- TalkinBroadway.com

"It's a little Paddy Chayefsky, a lot Neil Simon and a quick-witted, intelligent voyage into the not-so-tranquil seas of middle-aged love and dating. The dialogue is crackling and hilarious; the plot simple but well-turned; the characters endearing and quirky; and lurking beneath the merriment is so much heartache that you'll stand up and cheer when the unlikely couple makes it to the inevitable final clinch."
- NYTheatreWorld.Com

COCKEYED
William Missouri Downs

Comedy / 3m, 1f / Unit Set

Phil, an average nice guy, is madly in love with the beautiful Sophia. The only problem is that she's unaware of his existence. He tries to introduce himself but she looks right through him. When Phil discovers Sophia has a glass eye, he thinks that might be the problem, but soon realizes that she really can't see him. Perhaps he is caught in a philosophical hyperspace or dualistic reality or perhaps beautiful women are just unaware of nice guys. Armed only with a B.A. in philosophy, Phil sets out to prove his existence and win Sophia's heart. This fast moving farce is the winner of the HotCity Theatre's GreenHouse New Play Festival. The St. Louis Post-Dispatch called Cockeyed a clever romantic comedy, Talkin' Broadway called it "hilarious," while Playback Magazine said that it was "fresh and invigorating."

Winner!
of the HotCity Theatre GreenHouse New Play Festival

"Rocking with laughter...hilarious...polished and engaging work draws heavily on the age-old conventions of farce: improbable situations, exaggerated characters, amazing coincidences, absurd misunderstandings, people hiding in closets and barely missing each other as they run in and out of doors...full of comic momentum as Cockeyed hurtles toward its conclusion."
- Talkin' Broadway

NO SEX PLEASE, WE'RE BRITISH
Anthony Marriott and Alistair Foot

Farce / 7 m, 3 f / Interior

A young bride who lives above a bank with her husband who is the assistant manager, innocently sends a mail order off for some Scandinavian glassware. What comes is Scandinavian pornography. The plot revolves around what is to be done with the veritable floods of pornography, photographs, books, films and eventually girls that threaten to engulf this happy couple. The matter is considerably complicated by the man's mother, his boss, a visiting bank inspector, a police superintendent and a muddled friend who does everything wrong in his reluctant efforts to set everything right, all of which works up to a hilarious ending of closed or slamming doors. This farce ran in London over eight years and also delighted Broadway audiences.

"Titillating and topical."
- "NBC TV"

"A really funny Broadway show."
- "ABC TV"

www.ingramcontent.com/pod-product-compliance
Lightning Source LLC
Chambersburg PA
CBHW070630120726
47909CB00004B/1377